THE LEGACY SERIES

SERIES TITLES

This Is How We Speak
Rebecca Reynolds

I Felt My Life With Both My Hands
Jessica Treadway

Hands
Pardeep Toor

Lafferty, Looking for Love
Dennis McFadden

All That It Seems
Jim Landwehr

All Gone Now
Michael Tasker

Your Place in This World
Jake La Botz

Apple & Palm
Patricia Henley

Bodies in Bags
Jamey Gallagher

A Green Glow on the Horizon
Dawn Burns

How We Do Things Here
Matt Cashion

Neon Steel
Jennifer Maritza McCauley

Release of Information
Kali White VanBaale

The Divide
Evan Morgan Williams

Yes, No, I Don't Know
Kathryn Gahl

The Price of Their Toys
John Loonam

The Caged Man
Calvin Mills

A Day Doesn't Go By When I Don't Have Regrets
J. Malcolm Garcia

These Are My People
Steve Fox

We Should Be Somewhere by Now
Stephen Tuttle

Burner and Other Stories
Katrina Denza

The Plan of Chicago
Barry Pearce

Trust Issues
K.P. Davis

Adult Children
Laurence Klavan

Guardians & Saints
Diane Josefowicz

Western Terminus: Stories and A Novella
Michael Keefe

Like Human
Janet Goldberg

The Hopefuls
Elizabeth Oness

Never Stop Exiting
Michael Hopkins

Broken Heart Syndrome
Anne Colwell

The Mexican Messiah: A Novella & Stories
Jay Kauffmann

Close to a Flame
Colleen Alles

American Animism
Jamey Gallagher

Keeping What's Best Left Kept Secret
David Ricchiute

Soaked
Toby LeBlanc

The Path of Totality
Marie Zhuikov

Shocker in Gloomtown
Dan Libman

The Continental Divide
Bob Johnson

The Three Devils and Other Stories
William Luvaas

The Correct Response
Manfred Gabriel

Welcome Back to the World: A Novella & Stories
Rob Davidson

Greyhound Cowboy and Other Stories
Ken Post

Close Call
Kim Suhr

The Waterman
Gary Schanbacher

Signs of the Imminent Apocalypse and Other Stories
Heidi Bell

What We Might Become
Sara Reish Desmond

The Silver State Stories
Michael Darcher

An Instinct for Movement
Michael Mattes

The Machine We Trust
Tim Conrad

Gridlock
Brett Biebel

Salt Folk
Ryan Habermeyer

The Commission of Inquiry
Patrick Nevins

Maximum Speed
Kevin Clouther

Reach Her in This Light
Jane Curtis

The Spirit in My Shoes
John Michael Cummings

The Effects of Urban Renewal on Mid-Century America and Other Crime Stories
Jeff Esterholm

What Makes You Think You're Supposed to Feel Better
Jody Hobbs Hesler

Fugitive Daydreams
Leah McCormack

Hoist House: A Novella & Stories
Jenny Robertson

Finding the Bones: Stories & A Novella
Nikki Kallioy

Self-Defense
Corey Mertes

Where Are Your People From?
James B. De Monte

Sometimes Creek
Steve Fox

The Plagues
Joe Baumann

The Clayfields
Elise Gregory

Kind of Blue
Christopher Chambers

Evangelina Everyday
Dawn Burns

Township
Jamie Lyn Smith

Responsible Adults
Patricia Ann McNair

Great Escapes from Detroit
Joseph O'Malley

Nothing to Lose
Kim Suhr

The Appointed Hour
Susanne Davis

PRAISE FOR
This Is How We Speak

Rebecca Reynolds's *This Is How We Speak* introduces an outstanding writer whose stories will make you gasp, cry, smile, and most of all feel as you follow her characters through lives that are at once ordinary and, by virtue of the author's ability to render their hearts and minds with such grace and insight, extraordinarily poignant and real. We inhabit these mothers, lovers, sisters, daughters, and dreamers so completely that each leaves an indelible mark. Reynolds is the real deal, and this collection is a stunning debut.

—JESSICA TREADWAY
author of *I Felt My Life with Both My Hands*
winner of the Flannery O'Connor Award

Rebecca Reynolds's characters refuse to accept what they've been given: "I just wanted," one narrator says, "and wanting was a skill I'd perfected." Desire is at the heart of *This Is How We Speak*, present in the crunch of ice underfoot, the fat snowflakes melting on one's skin. These stories are vibrant and alive and necessary.

—MARY MILLER
author of *Always Happy Hour: Stories*

Don't let the quiet atmosphere of these thirteen tales fool you: each one is rife and ready with propulsive, dizzying tension. A mother tending to chickens in a snowstorm. A young woman training for a marathon with her father. A man visiting his step-brother in the hospital. With characters richly drawn and expertly detailed, Reynolds mines the depths of everyday experiences for the shocking turns and resolutions they allow to unfold.

—COLLEEN ALLES
author of *Close to a Flame*

this is how we speak

stories

rebecca reynolds

CORNERSTONE PRESS
UNIVERSITY OF WISCONSIN-STEVENS POINT

Cornerstone Press, Stevens Point, Wisconsin 54481
Copyright © 2026 Rebecca Reynolds
www.uwsp.edu/cornerstone

Printed in the United States of America.

Library of Congress Control Number: 2026930487
ISBN: 978-1-968148-38-6

All rights reserved.

This is a work of fiction. Names, characters, businesses, places, events, and incidents are either the products of the author's imagination or used in a fictitious manner. Any resemblance to actual persons, living or dead, or actual events is purely coincidental.

Cornerstone Press titles are produced in courses and internships offered by the Department of English at the University of Wisconsin–Stevens Point.

DIRECTOR & PUBLISHER	EXECUTIVE EDITORS
Dr. Ross K. Tangedal	Jeff Snowbarger, Freesia McKee
EDITORIAL DIRECTOR	SENIOR EDITORS
Brett Hill	Lhea Owens, Paige Biever

PRESS STAFF
Samantha Bjork, Sophie McPherson, Brianna Loving, Lilly Kulbeck, Aja Wooley, Lilli Resop, Christiana Niedzwiecki, Hannah Rouer, John Evans, Jazmyne Johnson, Andrew Bryant

For my parents

stories

Everyone Is Smiling   1

The Battle   7

Humane   21

The Natural World   32

Remember How I Loved You   45

Distance   57

Grace Period   72

Lucky   85

The Principle   97

The Visit   114

Dysfluency   126

Dinosaur   136

This Is How We Speak   150

Acknowledgments   161

Everyone Is Smiling

At low tide, Scylla is a blue mound rising from the beach. Ollie and JJ follow you closer, dragging their sneakers in the cold sand, bickering with each other. You have brought them here to see the whale. That they are not amazed, amazes you. You cannot take your eyes off the massive creature; you reach out your hand to feel the protrusion of her puckered, closed eye.

"Can you believe this?" you say.

"Why didn't they push her back in," Ollie, your youngest, says, his tone flat as if it is not a question. It is the same tone he uses to ask when you are coming back home.

JJ coughs twice, wedging the word *moron* in between. The cough-insult-cough schtick is new; last weekend it was *plead the fifth*, which was his answer to every question you asked about sixth grade, or his friends, or if he was going to try pitching another game in Little League. When you hug him, he keeps his arms at his sides. The boys are unsure about you, as if you are a stranger who is impersonating their mother. They are moody at your apartment and complain about the bubblegum pink walls and the cooking smells from your neighbors and your spotty Wi-Fi, but they do not cry around you. Like animals, they do not reveal injury in unfamiliar surroundings.

"They tried to," you say. "But she was too heavy." A few five-gallon buckets remain from the effort, stacked into a tower beside the whale's sunken jaw. A pair of onlookers stand at a distance, while a group of teenage girls takes selfies on the other side of the whale's body. For May it is cold, and in the rush to leave the apartment you have forgotten to bring jackets. Ollie and JJ drive their hands into their pockets, narrowing their frames into reeds, as they stand side by side, two dark-haired boys with the same dimpled chin, one a full head taller than the other. You try to ignore the wind's bite, awed by this implausible, misplaced body, the humpback's ridged flesh twisted as if paused in motion. Three days ago she beached and died. Now, she is an attraction.

"Let's take a picture," you say.

JJ steps back. "I'm pretty sure it can explode," he says. "You know, methane build-up, and whatnot. I saw it in a video. Gross."

"Is that true?" Ollie asks. He looks at his brother and then you, unsure which way to move. Last night he wet the bed and woke with a howl, begging for his father.

"Oh," you say, glancing at the whale. "I doubt it." This is the wrong answer. Though you do not share JJ's obsession with YouTube Shorts, you should know better than to hesitate when explosions are concerned. Both boys look at their feet, reminding you that you still have not learned how to be a proper mother. Eleven years later, and you are the same woman in the hospital bed, loopy from Percocet, who tried to give the crying baby back to the nurse.

"Why did you move here?" Ollie asked you last night, his knees showing under the college T-shirt you'd given him to change into, while you pulled wet sheets from the trundle bed in the guest room. You denied his requests to call his father, the man you were still married to, the man who took off his glasses and massaged the corners of his eyes and said *maybe you need to talk to someone* when you tried to explain yourself. A call home at 2:00 a.m. meant nothing less than failure on your part. And what could you say to Ollie in place of the truth? "I like it here," you tried, which was not a lie. You had not yet tired of the thrill each new day brought, the wide-open expanse of newness, hemmed in only by your worry for your children. But the real answer was your love for your boys was so heavy your chest ached to hold it, and still it wasn't enough because you wanted more.

Scylla was a mother, too. The article you read online said scientists have identified at least four of her calves. They have been tracking her for decades. Humpbacks can live to be ninety, you read, but Scylla was only middle-aged when she died. Forty-one. Your age. One day, instead of continuing her migration out into the feeding grounds of the Atlantic, Scylla separated from her pod and swam in the wrong direction until she ended up here, on this beach in Maine.

What is it about that age that can drive a whale onto land, can make you decide to leave your husband and children? The day you unpacked your carry-on in a coworker's friend's two-bedroom sublet that came furnished and decorated in a beach theme, you walked room to room with a glass of warm chardonnay, taking inventory of the wicker furniture, hotel-grade paintings, stenciled seashell wallpaper strips, thumping from the upstairs neighbors, and the odor of frying onions from next door and knew that you had actually done it—you had abandoned every real thing you had. And why? Because, as your husband accused, you would never be satisfied? Perhaps he was right; throughout fifteen years of marriage you had held nine jobs to his one, you were googling impossible vacations while he played *Sorry!* on the carpet with the boys. Restlessness grew in you like a virus. Sometimes you worried you'd pass it on to the boys, this inability to settle, and you couldn't help but wonder if they would be better off without you. In the end, all you knew was that you had been plowing, head down, through life.

When you finally broke away and looked up, the brightness was blinding.

"The whale is not going to explode," you say, trying again. "Okay?"

"I wouldn't rule it out," JJ says.

"Can we go?" Ollie asks. "I'm cold." You put your arm around him and feel his muscles quiver.

"We just got here. Don't you want to get a good look?" You want them to be impressed by this enormous creature before them, close enough to touch. You want it to mean something to them. You run your hand along the white edge of her fin. "Feel it," you say.

JJ folds his arms. "And get diphtheria? No thanks."

"Don't be afraid," you say. "Look." You point out the two blowholes on top of the whale and describe how whales must think about breathing, that it isn't involuntary like in people. You tell them how each tail fluke is as unique as a fingerprint. You show them the baleen peeking through the whale's mouth and explain she needed to catch over a ton of krill each day just to survive. You find it all fascinating, every detail of the article you read this morning still humming in your ears, but when you stop talking you turn to see Ollie and JJ gazing back at the car, kicking their toes into the sand. The group of teenage girls is walking away, huddling together.

"Okay, guys. One picture, then we'll leave."

With that, Ollie meets your eyes. "Are we going home?"

You become aware of the coldness in your fingertips and the tip of your nose. "Sure," you say, too quickly, a matter of habit. You squint into the breeze. "You mean back to my apartment? Or home to Daddy?"

JJ and Ollie lock eyes, transmitting a silent message. For all their fighting since the separation, the boys have forged a new connection you are not privy to. You find it both heartbreaking and heartening, this necessary bond. It is something that excludes you and therefore is something you cannot ruin. "Home means home," JJ says.

You lean a hip against the whale, feeling her damp coldness seep through your jeans, wishing you could stay here with her. When you leave, and everyone else goes home, tonight, she will be alone. "Alright," you say, unsure exactly what you are agreeing to, but certain it is not optional. With this, their shoulders rise. The promise of home strengthens them while it erases you.

Ollie picks up a rock and tosses it into the waves. "Daddy says you'll be back by summer," he says.

"Oh?"

JJ clears his throat. "He just said maybe, that's all."

"I see."

You know they are waiting for you to tell them you will leave your ugly apartment and move back home, that things will go back to the way they were. You know this is what a better mother would do. You have never lived on your own before, and you don't know how you are supposed to justify doing it so abruptly at this point in your life. Is it to find yourself? To finish your novel? To travel? You want all these things but none of them makes up for what you will lose. The world is so big, though, and you are hungry for it. You want, and you want, and you want. It is something you cannot seem to fix.

"Maybe," you say. "Maybe, by summer." The fact that struck you most while reading the article about Scylla was how female humpbacks whisper to their babies when they are small, so as not to draw predators to the vulnerable calves. To keep them safe. In this moment, you tell yourself that is what you are doing—not lying but whispering. In truth, you have already re-signed the lease. The thought of it tightens your throat.

"Hey, big smiles," you manage to say. You pull the boys beside you and hold your phone up, angling to capture the dead whale behind you.

JJ rolls his eyes but leans in, and on the phone's screen Ollie's dark gaze meets yours. In the background is the bulbous, white fin of Scylla. "There you go," JJ says, ventriloquist style, his lips stiff in a grin.

"Ollie, smile!" you say.

"Just take it," JJ says.

"You're not smiling."

"This is how I smile."

"Come on."

"I'm trying!"

"Cheese!" you say, and press the circle, the three of you pushed close, eyes lifted skyward. And then they are gone, running back toward the car, leaving you holding the phone in your outstretched arm. You tap the picture, focusing in and out, as if you do not trust the device to save the image in all its brilliance, as if the next time you take the phone out to look, their faces will have turned away, and it will only be you smiling into the sun. You will stare at this picture many times over the next year, and each time you will tell yourself it is proof the boys were, in this one moment, perfectly okay.

Waves have begun to wash over Scylla's tail fluke as the tide rises. Tomorrow, scientists will drag her back into the ocean and transport her body to a research facility where they can perform a necropsy. They will study her organs and blood, determine what killed her, what was to blame. What was she after, swimming so close to the shore? For her sake, you hope her last moments were fleeting and painless, that she did not have long to suffer the knowledge of her miscalculation. When sand rubbed against her belly and the last wave slipped over her dorsal fin, you hope she felt a momentary thrill at the vast, new land before her. You hope she, too, was blinded by the brightness.

The Battle

Helen should have prayed before they left. In the morning, toasting waffles and gathering shoes and packing a tote bag with juice boxes and Goldfish and baggies of orange segments she had meticulously cleansed of the bits of pith Anthony hated, there was no time. Rosie wanted to wear her Ariel costume, and it took Gerald half an hour to locate Anthony's musket in the backyard, where Anthony insisted he hadn't left it, under the trampoline. In the minivan, Helen belted herself in and then unbelted, remembering that she hadn't fed the cat, and once inside she crossed herself to see she had left the coffee maker on.

"We're going to be late," Helen said, as Gerald shifted into reverse. It was his first day off from the restaurant in weeks. Helen closed her eyes and tried to pray that he would get them to the reenactment on time, and also that Anthony's friends would be real, but she was too scattered, and the flurry of activity had left a pinch of nausea in the back of her throat. Anthony grabbed her headrest.

"My kepi cap! Did you get it, Mom?" he said. Rosie clapped her hands to her ears. Anthony was speaking in a Southern accent, as he had been doing recently when he talked about the new group of boys at school who, supposedly, let him sit at their table in the cafeteria. Helen's heart broke for him a little more every day. What he had gotten himself into today, with this Civil War reenactment meet-up he had found with the help of said new friends, Helen didn't know, and it didn't sit right with her.

"I got it, I got it," she said, straining against her seatbelt to reach the tote bag at her feet. She pulled out the gray, woolen hat with the black brim and gold buckle that Anthony had ordered from eBay.

"Oh, thank you Jesus," Anthony said.

Helen patted her hand at the air, the way she did to show Anthony he needed to tone it down. Anthony was not good at toning things down. He had no friends, unless you counted Ryder from down the street, whose father had a glass eye and probably a drinking problem and who, Helen suspected, was the one who hacked Anthony's Instagram account and put that disgusting picture on it. Helen had come close to calling Ryder's father, but Gerald said to leave it alone. Just go on, as if everything were normal. Helen prayed for that most of all, for Anthony to be normal, to finally achieve the anonymity of fitting in. She imagined it like a magic act, the waving of a wand and some sleight of hand, and then—*POOF*—Anthony would become so normal that he would disappear.

Now Anthony had the cap on backwards, making the peace sign into his phone, taking selfies. That was the hardest part for Helen, really: the worse things got, the more Anthony enjoyed himself.

Helen's nausea loosened into the emptiness of a growling stomach. She breathed in for four beats and out for eight, which she'd read online was a special combination if you wanted to become calm, though it made her lightheaded. Maybe that was the point, Helen thought. In the wooziness, she visualized herself filling with helium and floating away from the children and from Gerald, drifting over the silent trees. From that quiet place, Helen could watch her family as if she were watching a family on television, with mild interest and detachment. Anthony's strange and worrisome behavior would not drive a screw into her heart. But Helen didn't let herself drift for long. She resumed shallow breaths and organized a prayer list in her head, reanimating her anxiety. The worrying was what kept her feet on the ground. If Helen drifted too far, she didn't know if she would return.

HELEN PRAYED FOR HER FAMILY. She prayed for the restaurant. She said her prayers quickly and out loud each morning while Gerald was in the bathroom. Since his second operation, things had been pretty stopped-up for him, inside. Helen prayed for that, too.

Helen was specific when she prayed. This was something she considered a little trick-of-the-trade. When Anthony was in elementary school, she jotted bullet points on the back of the mortgage envelope while making dinner so she would not forget to pray for Anthony's ADHD medication to last through homework time, for his lowercase R's not to look like F's, for his working memory to strengthen and his dyslexia to sort itself out, and for him to stop hiding under the table when the tutor came. She prayed for them all to lose five pounds—that would be a start at least—and for Gerald's blood sugar to stabilize. She prayed that Rosie would stop doing that sassy thing that made the other girls call her Peppa Pig. She prayed that the summer slump at the restaurant wouldn't last past July, that the new pastry chef would stop showing up drunk. For the most part, Helen's prayers had been answered, in one way or another, although sometimes, despite her specificity, she wondered if God was toying with her, such as the time she prayed for Gerald to finally take a vacation from the restaurant and he ended up having a mild heart attack while driving home, winding him up in the hospital for a full weekend.

These days, Helen prayed for Anthony to fit in at middle school, and yet it seemed he was sticking out more and more. At eighth-grade orientation, touring the technology lab, Anthony would not stop pestering her for an Altoid, going so far as to snatch her purse away and hold it up, out of her reach. She stood on her tiptoes and batted at it several times before giving up. Anthony wore her purse on his shoulder, swaying as he walked in front of her, and offering Altoids to anyone who would glance his way, which was almost nobody. The more people ignored him, and the more embarrassed Helen got, the happier Anthony appeared to be. It was something Helen found incomprehensible; her entire life was built around the organizing principle of *do not draw attention*. She saw what happened to the people who singled themselves out, whether it was that poor red-headed boy from her elementary school whom all the kids laughed at for wearing his Boy Scout uniform every day of the week, and who died, horribly, at nineteen, of an undiagnosed case of strep throat, or that mom from CCD who never shut up about how fluoride was a neurotoxin and wasn't invited to the post-confirmation potluck so the other moms could complain about her. Helen saw herself as ordinary, and absolutely not special, and she conducted her affairs accordingly. And while, in her heart, she did believe her children were unique, amazing creatures, she was in no way compelled to thrust this belief on anyone else, which would have been an act of hubris, and punishable in all the ways hubris was routinely and mercilessly punished.

When the teacher asked if there were any questions, Anthony raised his hand.

"Do you have any Grey Poupon?" he asked.

Helen wanted to vanish. And, more than that, as guilty as it made her feel, she wanted Anthony to vanish.

"Excuse me?" the teacher said. Parents and students stared.

"I say, good lady, do you have any—"

"*Tony*," Helen said. She waved a hand at the teacher, motioning for her to move on. "It's nothing, a joke."

When Anthony came home the day after the Instagram debacle, saying that he hadn't sat with Ryder at lunch and had, instead, eaten with a new group of boys, Helen sensed something dodgy about it. She felt herself wanting to drift off into that quiet place. She did not want to imagine the ways this could play out for Anthony. Perhaps God had finally answered her prayers, but just in case she checked Anthony's phone after he went to bed. Most of the texts were nonsensical jokes he had sent to her and she had ignored, such as the one that said "Guess what? Chicken-butt!" The rest, also unanswered, were sent to numbers she didn't know, some of them just saying "HEYYY," the blue captions floating hopeful and alone at the top of the screen.

ANTHONY CRIED "BULLY!" at the sight of white tents in the field. They turned into Blackrock Senior Center, which the Junior Regiment registration form said marked the plot of land—nearly twenty acres of field and forest—where the 28th Volunteer Infantry staged its annual reenactment. Gerald drove slowly down a gravel path, toward a roped off section of grass where cars were parked, while Anthony cracked his knuckles.

Helen scanned the field. There were dozens of adult soldiers in blue uniforms, some around small fire pits and others talking and gesturing with gloved hands, and also women in old fashioned dresses with cinched waists and their breasts heaved up over the tops of their bodices, which made Helen look away. Soldiers took turns holding their rifles up to their eyes and aiming into the distance, firing shots that popped like firecrackers. There were civilians, too, other parents she guessed, lined up along the edge of the field with folding chairs and coolers as if they were at a soccer game or some other activity following norms Helen was familiar with, and this was modestly reassuring to her.

Rosie, who had fallen asleep on the drive, woke and began to whine. Her Ariel dress twisted around her leggings. "Now I'm hungry."

"Shut up, Rosie," Anthony said, poking her in her shoulder with his gun.

"Do not hit your sister!" Gerald shot back. He rubbed his hands together and looked at Helen. "You alright?"

Helen pulled the Goldfish bag from the tote and handed it back to Rosie. She met Gerald's eyes and nodded once, slowly. She was nervous for Anthony, and she had that feeling of remoteness as if she were still drifting a bit, pulling away from the emotional consequences that were soon to unfold. Let go and let God, she thought, picturing the flowery cross-stitch in the kitchen of the church basement, and yet she knew that required a level of trust in God that she did not quite have. God didn't take down the profile picture of two slick, nude men with Anthony's school picture Photoshopped onto the bent-over man's face. God didn't smite Ryder or even delay one of his father's disability checks. Helen steadied herself and turned to her son.

"Come with me," she said.

Clouds blocked the sun from providing any warmth. Helen tried to step over the wet places in the field, going as quickly as she could, though she could not keep up with Anthony who was several paces ahead, heading for the registration table.

The soldier standing behind the table saluted Anthony, his palm facing forward, and Anthony did the same. Helen searched her purse for the slip of paper. Her hands weren't working quite right; her fingers kept bumping into her wallet and getting hooked around her key ring.

"He's supposed to be in the Junior Regiment," Helen said. She unfolded the permission slip and worked out the creases against her chest. "There's a group of them? Is this the right place?"

"Affirmative," the soldier said, winking in Anthony's direction. The man turned to Helen, and she could see he had a kind, average face, probably a banker in his other life, or a dentist. He held the permission slip up in front of him as if checking to see if it were counterfeit, turning it one way and then the other, which made Helen nervous though she had printed the form herself, and had triple checked that she had filled it out correctly. He made a mark on a clipboard and clicked his tongue, then pointed to a tent across the field. "Head on over. They'll be waiting for you."

Helen looked at the tent. She could make out several other boys. And they were in gray uniforms!

"Those are your friends, then?" she asked Anthony. "Those boys over there?"

Anthony put a hand to his forehead and peered at the tent. "Yep, that's them," he said. He dropped his hand and grinned, facing Helen, and she began to fiddle with the brass buttons on his shirt.

"What are their names? Are they in your grade?"

"They're going to start without me," Anthony said, trying to pull away. Helen held on to his collar with one hand and rubbed away traces of breakfast from his cheek with the other. Was she sending him to the wolves?

"And you know what to do? They'll give you instructions?"

"Uh-huh," he said, his eyes on the tent. "I mean, we already figured it all out. I wrote the script myself. So, yeah, I guess I know what to do."

"There's a script?"

"Sure. I mean not with dialogue and stuff, just like, the positions. And who dies. Obviously."

Helen wished he'd let her see the script, in case there were errors or typos. Anthony was terrible at typing. And yet the idea of a script comforted her greatly. There was a plan. All Anthony had to do was follow it. "Oh, okay," she said.

"That's why they need me. They wanted me to do it."

Helen considered this and realized it made sense. Anthony had prepared the script in exchange for his place in it. She could see the social logic.

"Come on, Mom. I've got to get over there. It's going to start."

Helen let go of his collar and stepped back. His uniform appeared real when you weren't up close. "Okay," she said, though she reached out again, squeezing his upper arm.

"You're being weird. You know this is pretend. Right?"

Helen laughed, suddenly, and tightness released in her. She let the laughter come. Her chest shook and her eyes watered. She thought how silly she had been, how worried over nothing. Though it wasn't nothing—it was always something with Anthony—but maybe the something wasn't as heart-stoppingly bad as she'd worried it would be. "Go," she said, finally, taking a breath and blinking her eyes clear. She patted his cheek. "Don't make them wait."

Anthony jogged off toward the Junior Regiment tent, where the boys were forming themselves into lines and pretending to shoot each other. "My brothers!" Anthony shouted as he ran, and one boy turned and waved. Helen closed her eyes and felt the clouds part and let the sun through, as if someone had flicked on a light. She turned and walked to the edge of the field where Gerald stood, holding Rosie on his shoulders.

"He found his group," Helen said, making tiny, celebratory claps. Gerald nodded, and Helen saw that he had never doubted that there was a group, and so was not as pleased as she. For several moments they stood together in their own space, another pack in a line of family packs, the three of them gazing out over the muddy field. The soldiers retreated to their tents and corners of the field, and the Junior Regiment was not visible. In the lull, Rosie sat on Gerald's shoulders crunching Goldfish, Gerald rubbing the shins of her leggings, the hem of her dress bunched up behind his neck, and Helen prayed silently, trying not to move her lips. It was quick and rote, not much more than a list of complaints, truly, but when she prayed for Anthony she asked only that today would be a good day. She would leave the other items for another day so as not to distract God from the situation at hand. After amen, she added a thank you.

Rosie dropped her bag of fish to point. "Tony!" she squealed.

And there Anthony was, marching with his group out of the far corner of the field. Though they were a ways off, Helen could tell which one was Anthony because his steps were exaggerated and he was the only one swinging his arms in time with the marching. The others were already falling out of placement. They were four across and four deep, and an adult soldier trailed off to one side. Anthony was in the front row, and when the adult yelled a command, Anthony and the other three boys in front held their rifles to their eyes and shot, though their guns, per the rules, were non-firing unlike those belonging to the adults. They yelled "bang!"

Closer to Helen, near the front of the field, a group of blue soldiers shouted and marched forward, and several guns went off loudly, releasing authentic flashes. Just like that, the battle had begun. Gerald squinted at the field. The blue soldiers were everywhere now, so many of them. The boys were screaming and laughing and running; the formation had scattered. More gunshots, puffs of smoke hanging like smudges in the air.

"You see him?" Gerald asked.

Helen strained to look. She realized she could not find Anthony, though she could see the gray of the Junior Regiment members and the figures themselves, now darting and running in the grass. Which one was Anthony? Helen could not be sure, except to know that he was one of those frantic figures retreating from the line of blue soldiers. She caught on one and then jumped to another, but she lost him in the action or the glare. He was a part of the group, momentarily indistinguishable to Helen, which was something she had not experienced before. It was both disorienting and thrilling. Helen tried to relax into the sensation, as if giving in to the effects of a glass of wine. For once, she was not pulling Anthony back or shushing him; she could not even pick him out of the crowd.

Then, a scream. Helen's ears pricked at the sound of Anthony's voice rising from the thicket of boys. "They're after me!" he shouted, in his unmistakable accent, and Helen zeroed in, her brief tipsiness gone. There he was, in front of a stump that had a kettle on it, arms raised with his musket, which he held in one fist by the barrel, dangling by his head. The blue soldiers were surrounding him. "Save me Jesus!" His arms shook as he yelled. The blue soldiers, some of them full grown men, circled.

Where were the other boys? Helen stepped forward and held her hand to her eyes. Behind her, Gerald was blowing his nose and Rosie was pointing at her dropped Goldfish. Helen took another step, flattening the bag under her sneaker. Rosie shrieked. A blue soldier put a hand on Anthony's shoulder and pushed him to his knees.

"Let me go!" Anthony yelled. "Help me brothers!" His voice sounded higher than before, genuine. This didn't seem to be right; was this in the script that Anthony wrote? Why would he have chosen this ending for himself? The blue soldiers were closing in. One snatched Anthony's gun, another held Anthony's arms behind his back, and one was kneeling, funneling powder into his gun, which was not plastic.

She wanted to run to him, but that was wrong, she knew. Everyone would think she was a loon, as if she didn't know that a reenactment was only acting, playing around. Anthony's screams wrenched her. She hugged herself and looked down, away from the action. She was going there, to the quiet place. Her breathing slowed and her body relaxed, and she felt the tightness in her chest, that painful, impossible need to control everything and to hold it all in her hands, loosen as if she were rising up from the water and taking a breath. Let go and let God. Just let Him deal with this for a while. She was so tired. She hadn't always been a mother; she had been her own, separate person, once, though that was lifetimes ago. She wanted to sit down on the grass like a child and put her head in her hands.

Then she heard the cry. Anthony's cry—not a scream but a sob, a real sob, the whine and the choppy bawl. "Oh, mama!" he cried.

"Did you hear that?" she said to Gerald.

"What?" Gerald was trying to refold his hanky without letting go of Rosie's legs.

"Oh," Helen said. "It's him. Something's wrong."

Gerald sniffed. "It's war, hon," but Helen was already jogging into the field. The other parents had to be staring; she could feel it. She hated jogging in front of people, the jolting heft of her body. She hated the looks. The battle moved on, spreading out across the grass, some of the soldiers running past her close enough for her to hear their breaths, and Helen hoped she would blend into the movement, though she acknowledged the silliness of this thought even as she had it.

"Mercy, men! Mama, oh mama!" Anthony cried. Three blue soldiers had stayed behind with him. They were laughing at him, two of them small but one tall enough to be a father, and even he was laughing. Helen ran, flushing hot with the pulse of her blood. She was running as she did when Anthony was small and would fall and hurt himself, even though he would push her away, would slap at her as she comforted him. She was running as she did when he was in first grade and thought it was hilarious to ride his bike down the middle of the street when a car was coming, and as she did just weeks before when she had chased him down and pried the phone from his hands to see what had happened to his Instagram account. She would always be running after Anthony. A blue soldier fired a smoky shot and Anthony clutched at his chest and screamed as if he were in real pain, not pretend, but true and sorrowful pain. Then he fell on his face in the mud. The blue soldiers scattered.

When Helen reached him, Anthony lay on his stomach in the damp grass, his face turned away. He was moaning and grunting, in the death throes. The game had moved on, and nobody was coming back for her son. Not his friends, or brothers, or whatever they were, if they were anything at all. What Helen knew was that she had momentarily given the wheel to God, and He had driven them off a cliff. God was there, perhaps, but He was not merciful. That was left to the mothers.

"Anthony!" she said. "Get up! Are you hurt?"

Anthony rolled onto his back and Helen saw his face was smeared with dirt. "Oh my," she said. She reached for him. He was quiet now, his breath coming in pants, and as he turned to her, Helen saw his eyes were moist and reddened, but the grin on his face was ecstatic.

"Did you see it?" he whispered.

"Of course! You died!"

"I got to be the first one."

There were others lying dead on the field, now, Helen saw them accumulating with each pop and puff of gunpowder. "You scared me," she said. "I thought they were hurting you."

"Nah."

Boys and men crumpled over each other, some lying on their backs with gruesome expressions on their faces, one draped over a pile of firewood. Some were screaming. None of their mothers had run to them. What had Helen been thinking? She had made a fool of herself. She didn't want to turn around and face Gerald and the others.

Anthony wiped his nose with his sleeve. "You have to go back. What if they see you?"

Helen knew it was too late to worry about that. "You were crying for me," she said.

"I was acting."

"But I believed you."

Anthony grinned, mud drying on his chin. "I thought it was good. I bit my cheek hard to get real tears." To prove his point, Anthony spit a wad of bloody saliva onto the grass next to Helen. "See?"

Helen nodded absently, finding it hard to assimilate this information. "So, you're really alright?"

"Mom."

Helen began to drift. She had been certain, so very certain, that Anthony needed her, and he did not. She was wrong. And here she was, attracting attention for all the wrong reasons and ruining Anthony's special day. Anthony was okay, which she would not have thought possible a few minutes before. He was more than okay; she saw this now. Though she was mortified and sweaty and had no idea how she would stand up and walk back to her family with any dignity at all, Anthony was completely and perfectly himself, and he was fine. She did not need to save him. She did not need to do anything. This, suddenly, felt wondrous to her, as if she could let go of her worries and become lighter than air, as if she really could float up and away from the scene. It was so freeing, the lightness, so hard to fight. She knew she shouldn't give in to it. What would happen then? What would happen if she floated too far?

Anthony rolled his head to glance at the other soldiers. "I'm supposed to be dead."

"I know." She gave his hand a squeeze that did not loosen. The ground had made her knees cold and wet; when she stood her pants would be muddy. She wanted to stay close to Anthony, but she was starting to lift off, as if she were filled with helium. Inside, where she once held her own fears and worries along with everyone else's fears and worries, there was now only an inert, colorless gas that was making it difficult for her to remain on the ground. Gravity was failing her. What would her family think when they saw her sailing in the wind like a kite? Would they miss her? Would they?

Anthony closed his eyes. "You better go." He twisted his hand and tried to slip from her grasp.

"I will," Helen said. She gripped harder. "I promise, I will." But she didn't move. She didn't dare make any motion at all. She tethered herself there, holding tight to her son, waiting for a break in the battle.

Humane

Andy drives with his left hand on the wheel and the right on the shifter, his thumb pushing the button on the side of the stick as if he is fighting the urge to see what would happen if he dropped it into reverse. His Honda is covered in PETA and animal welfare stickers including one that says *Kale yeah, I'm vegan!* I am next to him, essential oil bottles tinkling at my feet. Aside from the dashes of gray in Andy's hair, I could believe no time has passed since we were last in a car together, speeding toward the coast, nine years ago.

I was his wife then.

The summer after college, Andy drove thirteen hundred miles from our Tennessee campus to my parents' home in Maine, messing with the gearshift the whole way, so I guess it's safe to say this is how Andy acts when he is nervous about having to do something terrible.

Behind me, Andy's boyfriend sits with their cat. Back home in Sacramento, Dennis works as a veterinary technician. The cat is swaddled in a hospital grade blue and white striped blanket as if it were a newborn baby, and Dennis holds it like a football in the bend of his flannelled arm.

"We wanted Rudy to see everything," Andy says, accelerating around a bend. His eyes flash from the road to me as he describes the bucket-list road trip the three of them have been on for the past month. "Niagara Falls freaked him out a little, but he definitely appreciated Strawberry Fields." Rudy, the cat, has a spinal tumor, as well as congestive heart failure. He wears a diaper and must be carried by Dennis in a BabyBjörn infant carrier. He was originally Dennis' cat, but Andy is all in, which I'd like to tell Dennis has nothing to do with him, it's just something Andy does.

Andy and I started dating the week of freshman orientation. We married, just the two of us and not even a ring, at town hall a month after graduation. It was Andy's idea, something that came to him at 3:00 a.m. when he was too wired for sleep, fixated on a problem of which I was still unaware. Marriage had made sense; Andy already spent his college summers in Blue Hill with me, getting drunk on coffee brandy, kayaking with my dad, and raking blueberries for a week in August so he didn't have to ask his parents for gas money to drive back to school. I thought it was love that made him want to spend so much time with me and my family, but now I see Andy has an emptiness he tries to fill up with other people's lives. And other people's dying pets.

In the back seat, Dennis lifts the cat to his shoulder as if burping a baby. He strokes Rudy and hums into his ear, Dennis' dark beard blending into the cat's fur. "You're my good boy," he says.

"I'm glad you could come," Andy says, tilting his head in my direction. A week ago, he messaged me, explaining the odd request. Though I could think of excuses—my job, for one—I replied that I would be available. Part of me had been waiting nine years to see him again, to prove to myself that I hadn't imagined our whole relationship. "I'd never be able to find the beach on my own," he adds.

"Sure," I say. "I haven't been there in years, though." It was a rocky beach down an unmarked road, accessible only during good weather. The steely water produced sea foam that dried in tufts and stuck to the bottoms of your feet; when the tide went out, the seaweed clumps smelled fishy. I'd only ever seen dogs swim there. There was no shortage of more beautiful beaches in the area, but Andy and I preferred this one because nobody else did. Even on the hottest days, we had the place to ourselves. I read paperbacks in my bra. Andy would make cairns out of the largest beach stones, building towers that reached his chest. He tried to construct them solidly, to survive the tides, though they never did.

"This won't be easy," Andy says.

"No," I say. But I am thinking of myself, not the cat. Nothing about seeing Andy again is easy.

I turn away because I don't want Andy to see the color in my cheeks. Though I hoped enough time had passed for my feelings to harden, I am still attracted to him. In college, Andy had the kind of looks that got him free beer at parties and convinced his professors to allow extensions on his papers. The plan, after our three-minute wedding, was for me to spend the summer with my parents, saving money, while Andy finished his overdue senior thesis and applied to graduate programs in Maine, and at the end of the summer he would join me, and we'd find an apartment near the university. But instead, Andy drove away and disappeared from my life.

He didn't answer my calls or texts. In the evenings, after dinner, I would say I was waiting for Andy to call and would go to my room and lock the door, so my parents wouldn't ask questions. They weren't thrilled with the marriage in the first place. It made me sick, the not knowing. I ate peanut butter cups compulsively, woke up in the night with my T-shirt cold with sweat. When I finally did get a message, the night of my parents' Labor Day cook-out, it wasn't even from him. It was one of Andy's friends, whom I vaguely recalled from a logic class we had taken together. Cam admitted he had been sleeping with Andy for most of the past year. He added lots of pensive face emojis, repeating he was sorry, that they should have told me earlier and they didn't think it would amount to anything, but it had. Andy felt awful, but he wasn't ready to talk. I remember the smell of grilled chicken and bug-spray coming through my window, and how I texted LOL, at first, thinking he had to be kidding. Cam wrote, "Are you okay Lynne? Are you going to be okay?" and I couldn't think of anything to say aside from "NO." I turned off notifications and got into bed with my clothes still on and slept until noon the next day.

ANDY AND I TRADE SUMMARIES of the past nine years: I talk about my job in the special education room at the middle school, and my dad's cancer scare. I throw in a boyfriend or two to deflect pity, though in truth there's been too many to count, and none worth naming. After the break-up, my parents handled our annulment, their relief turning to solicitousness, telling me that everybody makes mistakes when they are young. But I hadn't felt that Andy was a mistake. I loved him. It was the first time in my life I was completely wrong.

Andy rushes through a list of past addresses and jobs. After six months with Cam, he moved west, away from his family and everyone he had known. He ended up at an organic bakery in Sacramento where he got a job making vegan donuts, which was where he met Dennis. "The first time I went over for dinner, Rudy peed on my shoes," Andy says. Dennis shifts the cat onto his lap and smiles.

When we were together, Andy planned to obtain his doctorate in philosophy. His father said it was a waste of money, but Andy wanted to be one of those hip young professors who makes cameo appearances at off-campus parties and organizes study sessions at coffee shops.

Now he is in an online school for animal aromatherapy.

"Essential oils are amazing stuff, just amazing," Andy says. He nods at the bottles rolling around my feet. "I've seen lavender oil cure a nasty case of sarcoptic mange."

"But not for cats," Dennis says.

Andy rolls his eyes. "Okay, really? You just had to bring that up."

Dennis laughs. "Oh, honey," he says.

Andy flashes me an embarrassed look. His cheeks are waxy and smooth, nicely bronzed. The shadow of hair below his lower lip is enough to remind me of kissing him. Afterwards, everyone asked me, couldn't I tell he was gay all along? Wasn't there some giveaway? The truth is we didn't have a lot of sex, and when we did it didn't seem as important as the place it brought us to, where Andy would fall asleep with his chin in the crook of my neck, his frenetic body finally still.

"Yeah, so, as it turns out most essential oils are toxic to cats, which okay, I did not exactly know when I signed up for this program," Andy says.

"He thought he would learn something that might save Rudy," Dennis says. He wipes his eyes. The cat yawns, exposing toothless black gums. "Damn, it was sweet."

Andy reaches a hand back between the seats and touches Rudy's blanketed body. Andy's hands were always clean, his fingernails cut just above the quick and softly rounded, his touch warm and dry on my skin. Once, Andy touched me with the care he is now touching Rudy. The cat squirms and arches his back, and suddenly the smell of fresh shit fills the car. Andy cracks his window. "Poor baby," he says.

"Here. After the mailboxes," I say, pointing. We turn off the main street and bounce over the rutted gravel road. Andy drives too fast, and the glass bottles at my feet threaten to break, but he shows no sign of concern. His face is bright, taking in the once familiar landscape. The last time Andy and I were here, he built rock towers around me like a jail.

There is a mist over the beach. We come to an abrupt stop along the side of the road, Andy and I opening our doors and quickly escaping the stink of the car. The wind is sharp. A line of seaweed stretches across the rocky shore. Andy raises his bare arms into the breeze and grins. "It's exactly how I remembered."

Dennis takes several moments to put a new diaper on the cat, then emerges from the car with Rudy zipped up inside his fleece-lined flannel jacket. Rudy's small head pokes out above the collar. Andy dutifully lifts the back of Dennis' jacket and latches the BabyBjörn, pulling the cinch tight around Dennis' waist. "You were right," Dennis says, taking in the area. He rotates to give Rudy a view. "It's beautiful."

The tide is out far enough for us to walk where the rocks have been worn to smaller pebbles, each one pushing into the soles of my flats. Dennis goes first, then Andy, and I fall back. The wind blows too strongly for conversation. We walk in silence the length of the beach, Dennis occasionally stopping to point something out to Rudy: a speckled juvenile seagull, a cargo ship passing across the horizon, the claw of a crab. Andy takes pictures with his phone. I stay out of the background. Last week, when Andy asked if I was able to join them in saying goodbye to their pet, it felt something like finding out my husband was having an affair with his buddy, like a riddle I couldn't quite parse. "Are you sure you want me to come?" I had typed back, trying to figure out exactly what was going on in Andy's head. "I'm not exactly a cat person."

"I've never been there without you," he responded. "And don't worry. Rudy is not exactly a cat."

I follow them up the beach to a patch of spruce. Close to the trees, we are sheltered from the wind. Andy puts his arm around Dennis, and Dennis nods.

"We're going to feed him, now," Andy says.

Dennis takes a small zip-top baggie from his pocket and pulls out what appears to be a sardine, which he places on Andy's cupped palm. Andy moves his hand under Rudy's chin, pinching a piece of the oily fish between his fingers and touching it to Rudy's lips. "Come on, baby," Andy says. The cat turns his head and flicks his tongue.

"Let me try," Dennis says. Andy transfers the fish to Dennis. Again, Rudy refuses.

"It's like he knows," Andy says.

Dennis shakes his head. Rudy sneezes.

"Lynne, why don't you try?" Andy says, looking at Dennis. Dennis offers me the fish.

"Oh, I don't think he's hungry," I say.

"He might take it from you," Dennis says. "With us, he thinks we're trying to sneak him a pill."

Feeding Rudy feels like unnecessary torture, for both the cat and me. But I reach out my hand. The fish is still warm from Dennis' pocket, and it flakes apart in my fingers. Rudy sniffs it, and then licks. Andy's face explodes with joy. Another lick.

"You've got the touch," Dennis says.

DENNIS AND RUDY GO DOWN TO THE WATER, and Andy and I walk back to the car, my hair blowing in all directions. Inside the Honda, the absence of wind feels warm. The smell of cat shit lingers. "Thanks for doing this," Andy says. His hair, as always, is perfect.

"Sure. Pretty normal way to spend an afternoon."

Andy smiles, taps his fingers on the steering wheel. "Well, I know it's weird." He turns to face me, the smile dropping. "Driving cross-country for a cat. You probably think I'm crazy."

I say nothing. Andy drove cross-country for me every summer and Christmas through college.

His thigh jiggles. "Sometimes I feel crazy, I really do. Like if I pinch myself I'm going to wake up, and I don't want to. We're happy together, me and Dennis. He makes me want to be better."

"He seems like a nice guy," I say, which isn't a lie.

"He's taught me a lot. I can't believe I used to eat meat without even thinking about it. When Dennis and I met, I told him I was a vegan. And then I ran home and threw out all the meat and eggs and milk in my fridge."

When we were together, Andy's favorite food was clam chowder that he would buy in cans and eat with Ritz crackers, the way my dad did. "I'm sure Dennis wouldn't care that you used to eat meat," I say.

"I'd never tell him."

I laugh. "What? Why not?"

Andy lifts his foot to the seat and begins to busy himself with the laces of his boot. "It's not important. This is who I am, now."

"Okay, sure," I say. Down by the water, Dennis crouches to pick something up, then tosses it into the waves. "Does he know about me?"

Andy pulls the laces tight and rubs a scuff on the toe. A gust of wind whistles around the car. "I said we went to college together. I didn't want to scare him, okay? This is about Rudy."

Heat floods my body. The feelings I've held close are loosening, years of questions pushing through my skin. "Is that why you didn't tell me about Cam? Because you didn't want to scare me?"

Andy puts his foot down and gathers himself, his hands on his knees. "I was going through a lot back then."

"Yeah," I say.

"And I'm sorry."

"I know." He has said it before, during calls when all I could do was mumble, *okay, okay*. I'm not sure if he is sorry because he loved me or because he didn't, or if it makes any difference. "Every memory I have of those years is like the build up to a joke I wasn't in on."

"There was no joke," Andy says.

"But there was," I say. "It just wasn't very funny."

"Oh, Lynne." He puts a hand to my face, his dry palm cupping my cheek. I rest into his touch. The feeling is warm and comforting. He leans closer, or at least I think he does, and I push off the seat and wrap my arms around him, my body leaning over the gearshift awkwardly, my toes knocking the oil bottles into each other. I know I shouldn't be doing this, but it's already too late. Andy lets me hold him, though he stiffens. The soapy scent of his hair gel hasn't changed. He pats my back, his hand flat against my jacket, turning his face away from mine. For a moment I fight the urge to kiss his cheek, to taste his skin one last time. As I pull away, a strand of my hair sticks to the stubble under Andy's lip.

I sit back down. My cheeks burn.

"It's cool," he says. He removes the hair. If I had any questions about Andy's feelings toward me, I don't anymore. I look out my window. For several breaths, we are silent.

"Lynne, you were the only thing that got me through college," Andy says, softly. "Your family, too. You have no idea what that meant to me, hanging out on the patio and grilling with your dad. I haven't talked to my own father in five years, since I told him about Dennis." Andy's mom used to force his father onto the phone when she called Andy, and if I listened closely, I could hear her voice in the background telling Andy's father to please just say something. Afterwards, Andy's always-fidgeting body would go quiet, as if he had decided to leave it for a little while.

I turn back to Andy, my face still warm. "Why did you come here?"

"I don't know. I told Dennis I would find the right place for Rudy. The perfect spot. I mean, Lynne, I didn't know where I was going, really. I just kept driving." When he laughs, his eyes glint.

Dennis turns around and moves up the beach, toward the car. I can't see Rudy's head from this distance, though I know he is there from the bulge in Dennis' jacket. I imagine how protected the cat must feel, hidden like that against another body.

"Dennis wants to get married. When we get back."

I tighten my cheeks into a shaky smile. "Oh. Congratulations."

Andy dabs at his eyes with the cuff of his sleeve. "Yeah. I mean, I thought you should know."

"Is that what you want, too?" I ask, my voice small, as if the question is about us, as if I am still trying to figure out what it is that Andy truly wants. I wonder if Andy actually knows. I can picture him driving across the country, telling Dennis the right spot for the cat is probably in the next town, the next state, and yet on some level knowing his only plan is to just keep driving. Eventually, he ran out of road.

"I think so," he says. "I love Dennis. I really do."

"I thought you loved me," I say before my better sense kicks in, and then, realizing what I said, I try to laugh. "But I guess that was different."

Andy looks at Dennis who is almost to the car. The wind has picked up, and Dennis' beard is being blown violently to one side. I want to touch Andy, but Dennis is too close, and Andy is too far away. The feeling is familiar and sad. None of this is about me, really, and yet here I am, wanting to change the unchangeable. I probably should have ignored Andy's message, let him think I no longer checked that account, that my life was too full and figured out for such things.

"No, not different." He looks me straight on, his attention like the towers he built, intense but fleeting. "Love is love, Lynne," he says. "It's simpler than you think."

"Well, it shouldn't be," I say, but Dennis has opened the car door, and the cold wind swallows my words.

THEY SET UP ON A BOULDER not far from the car; it has a flattened top so Dennis can prepare the syringes without needing to squat on the ground. Andy asks me if I want to come, but I decline. Alone in the car, I run my fingers through the rat's nest in my hair, anticipating the hot shower I will take when I get home.

The sky is growing pink. From my seat in the car, I watch Dennis carefully unzip his jacket. Andy detaches the clasp of the BabyBjörn and lifts Rudy's body and pulls the cat to his chest. Rudy's tail hangs in a crimped curve below Andy's arms. Dennis fills a syringe. He leans to kiss the cat between his ears, then takes a front leg and kisses his paw, too, before injecting the shot.

As Dennis prepares another syringe, Andy presses his face into Rudy's belly. When Andy left me at my parents' house, before he got into his car to drive away, he rested his chin on my shoulder and let my hair cover his face. I had hugged him, trusting as Rudy, no understanding of what was to come.

Dennis administers the second shot with professional swiftness. He secures the needles in a plastic container, and puts his arms around Andy and Rudy, hugging them both into his thick, flannel embrace. They hug so tightly that Rudy must already be dead, or else they would be concerned about suffocating him. Dennis' shoulders are shaking. I am relieved to be in the car, removed from the emotion. Behind the two men, the sunset is spreading out over the water. The image could be lovely.

They put Rudy's body into a quilted sack and lay the sack on the rock, and Dennis rests his hand on it, staring out at the reddening horizon. Andy bends and begins stacking rocks. Perhaps they have both forgotten about me, which is probably for the best. I am not part of the moment. At this point, my sympathies are with the cat. Rudy must have wondered what all the fuss was about, having to leave his home and travel from place to place. He couldn't have known it was a one-way trip. He had been so loved, and there was never any reason to be afraid.

The Natural World

The blizzard began in the morning. The boys were irritable with me, as they tended to be when their father was gone. It was Monday, and Teddy had left before dawn, driving four hours south to Boston to his job and a studio apartment I had never seen. During our weekdays, alone together in this Maine house where hours stretched between passing cars and contact with the outside world was limited to bi-weekly grocery runs, Micah and the baby cried and fought more, battled for the iPad during Teddy's nightly Facetime calls, and rose from naps, groggy and cross, asking where Daddy was. I believed they blamed me for his absence.

By lunch time, I'd spent too long sitting on the couch, staring at the fat snowflakes sticking to the window screen, while the boys watched Netflix on the iPad. I went to the kitchen, put bagels into the toaster and opened a Costco-sized can of mandarin oranges, draining off the sugary liquid. When Teddy was away, my parenting strategy was to placate, to feed the boys waffles and popsicles as if they were lions I could stupefy with gluttony, to skip tub time until the creases in the baby's elbows grew eczematic. Some days, I'd let them watch one movie after another so I could curl into my chair and read antique National Geographics left behind in the basement by the previous owner of our house, moisture-stiffened magazines that smelled of mothballs and were full of the wonders of nature—Jane Goodall's chimpanzees, undulating kelp forests, the language of elephants. It wasn't that I didn't adore my children, but routine details escaped me. Micah's bangs were so long he'd taken to holding them back with his hand when looking at something, but I put off finding a barber. I could not remember where I put the thick kindergarten packet that came in the mail which I was supposed to fill out to register him for school next year, though it was nearly due. When Teddy suggested it might help to have the boys spend some time with his mother, I asked if he thought I was incapable of caring for my own children, which brought us both to silence. We tried not to have those talks in front of the boys.

"Picnic time," I said, placing food on the living room carpet.

"Picnics are supposed to be outside," Micah said. He pushed back his bangs so I could see the incredulity in his eyes.

"They can be anywhere," I said. "Can't they?" Micah was my thinker, my studious child. He rarely smiled, but when he did it was because some idea in his mind had clicked into place. I liked to read the National Geographic articles to him when he'd let me. His favorite was about the death zone of K2, the highest region of the mountain in which there was not enough oxygen for humans to survive. In that place, the brain stopped working. Mountaineers had been known to take off all their clothes and freeze to death, nearly instantly.

"Maybe," Micah said, sitting. He and his brother fished orange wedges out of the bowl, sucked cream cheese, and wiped their fingers on pajamas I had not yet attempted to wrangle them out of. I sat with them, snatching up their bits of refuse. I knew I should eat proper meals, and yet I could not bring myself to bother. In my head I was writing a diet book called "The Scavenger's Guide to Weight Loss," which centered on consuming only the half-chewed remains from your toddler's plate, a satire. I was always writing books in my head, though I hadn't touched my laptop in weeks. I tried to tell Teddy about the idea over the weekend, but when spoken out loud it sounded more sad than funny, and Teddy had not understood to laugh, asking instead how my novel was coming. And for that I had no answer.

Outside, the wind shifted, buffeting the front of the house like a tidal wave. Micah jumped up to look out the window, flipping the bowl and spilling orangey syrup on the carpet. The baby sneezed bagel bits and cried out. The room, which had been peaceful, filled with chaos. I felt the desire to bolt through the front door, out into the howling storm.

It was my idea, of course, to move here. When COVID hit last year, our apartment in the city became unbearably claustrophobic, with Teddy working from the bedroom and the boys and I confined to a galley kitchen and living room, trying to be quiet for Teddy's work calls. We didn't go outside. We avoided confined spaces like the elevator. I ordered everything on Amazon, and the packages I sprayed with Lysol. I scrolled Zillow compulsively, dreaming of a cabin in the woods, a safe den where I could nurse my cubs. I wanted to escape with them, away from our apartment building with the sounds of coughing through the walls, the quarantine-empty streets, into the openness of nature. I wanted to watch my boys run barefoot and gather eggs and climb trees and pick wildflowers and hold fireflies in their cupped palms. I wanted to sit on a porch lit by strung globe lights and write books. But mostly, I just wanted, and wanting was a skill I'd perfected. In our nine years together, Teddy had known me to jump from one plan to another, from hope to hope, but even he could not argue with the logic of leaving.

We paid far too much for this house, a red saltbox on four acres. We moved last spring. Right away I bought a dozen chicks for the shed out back—a lovely breed, Orpingtons, fat and fluffy, dandelion yellow. The boys and I loved watching them grow, the way they knew to scratch and peck and roost themselves at dusk right on schedule, led by natural mechanism. We were happier, I think, all of us, away from the city. I could breathe. Then, in the fall, Teddy's office unexpectedly reopened. Suddenly, working remotely was no longer an option for him, and neither was the pay cut he would take by accepting a position locally. So here we were, five days a week living in different states, waiting either for the housing market to rebound so we could recoup our money, or for a miraculous industrial design job to open up within a fifty-mile radius. In short, the boys were right, this was my fault. Still, I could not get enough of the wild here, the crying coyotes, the way the night sky opened wide to the universe, each star winking its ancient light.

"Come here," I said to the baby, scooping him up and bringing him to the couch, feeling his wet face on my neck. He smelled of heat and diapers, and I checked to see if he needed to be changed but the diaper was still crinkly. I could not remember if I had given him any juice for breakfast. I lifted my shirt to let him nurse, though he was one and a half and mostly weaned. He turned away to breathe and mucus bubbled from his nostrils.

"I'm bored," Micah said. He picked up the dead iPad from the floor, tapped the black screen, and looked at me.

I pushed a fleet of Hot Wheels cars from the cushion next to me and patted it. "I'll put a movie on," I said. We'd been making our way through the stash of VHS tapes left in the house, my favorites being "Bambi" and "Dumbo," perhaps because both had mothers who were tragic, mammalian figures. I related, somehow. My love for the boys was sharp, serrated by the guilt I was failing them. At times, I wished they could be like my motherless hens, cracked from the egg with all the information required for survival.

"We already did that," he said, politely, as if perhaps I'd forgotten that fact. The baby was damp and limp in my arms, asleep, his mouth open. I thought of the afternoon ahead, the hours existing in one room and then another, trying to keep the boys happy, and felt exhausted.

"Yes, that's right." I nodded at a National Geographic lying on the couch, one with a mother elephant and her baby, in silhouette, on the cover. "Want to read with me?"

Micah shook his head and went back to the dead iPad, pressing the home button repeatedly as if that might revive it. Wind whistled through the chimney, and I realized I had let the hot coals from Teddy's fire last night go out. My earlobes were cold.

"Can you do a job for Mommy?" I asked.

"Okay," Micah said. "What is it?"

"Turn the heater on."

"Fine," he said, clearly dismayed, but he went to the baseboard and twisted the dial anyway. The element popped with energy. "That was easy. I want something hard."

It was then that I thought of my chickens. Several weekends back, I'd asked Teddy to hang a heat lamp over the shed rafters so I could run the extension cord out and plug it in when the temperature fell below twenty degrees. They were, quite literally, spring chickens, and this being their first winter I did not know what their tolerance for cold would be. It excited me, this thought of getting outside, away from the house, if only for a moment. I could be quick. I could do it before the baby woke up from his nap.

"Okay," I said, easing myself out from under the baby. I tucked him into the crease of couch cushions with a blanket. "Here's a hard job, then. I need you to watch your brother while I go check on the chickens."

"You're leaving?" Last weekend, at dinner, Micah told Teddy that I'd left to fetch mail from our mailbox and was gone so long Micah thought the coyotes had gotten me. "Coyotes don't attack people, bud," Teddy had told him quickly, patting him on the back while fixing his eyes on me. We both knew that was not the answer Micah was looking for.

"I'm not leaving. I'm going to the shed. It will take one minute, I promise." I thought of the blizzard outside, the way it would feel to be enveloped by that force, to have the wind twist around me like something alive. I had always been drawn to storms. "I need you to sit right here, and make sure your brother is alright. And you can't move, not until I get back. You have to sit completely still. You have to be a statue."

"Do I get a dollar?" Micah continued to eye me with scrutiny, bangs held back, but I could see the wheels in his head turning.

"Sure. A dollar." I could have promised him thousands; he still had little understanding of what the bills were, and anyway, the only store that had toys was Target in Bangor, and that was over an hour away.

"Three?"

"Okay, three dollars," I said. I ruffled his bangs and watched them fall back into his eyes. He hopped onto the couch and assumed a stiff position, hands on his lap. He concentrated. He was so careful not to move.

OUTSIDE, SNOWFLAKES STUNG my cheeks and the icy air in my lungs made me giddy with cold. At once, I felt awake. Teddy had left the yellow extension cord and a stepladder by the back door, and I took the cord but left the ladder, as it would be difficult to carry so far. I plugged the cord into the outlet box at the top of the steps and let it unwind behind me as I made my way to the shed, jogging in the snow. Near the shed, I paused, planted my feet, and tilted my head back, a trick I remembered from childhood. Looking up into the falling snow gave me the most pleasant vertigo, as if I could not tell if the snowflakes were zooming toward me or me to them, and I had the sensation of falling upwards into the sky, soaring through space. I let the feeling build until it was almost too much to bear. I righted my head and brushed the flakes from my eyes, taking in the white expanse. Tomorrow, I would bring the boys out to build forts and snowmen.

Inside the shed, it was dim except for light that came in through the cracks around the door and the gaps in the roof. My hens were roosted in pairs, feathers fluffed out over their scaly toes. As chicks, Micah had named each one, but now they were impossible to tell apart.

"Don't worry, ladies," I said. "I'll get this hooked up." The hens cooed. Their round eyes were half closed. They gave no indication of being chilled, though my fingers and toes were starting to throb a bit. I'd thrown on a jacket but no hat or mittens. The snow on top of my hair began to melt and trickle onto my scalp.

The heat lamp hung over a beam, secured by a knot in its cord, the plug several feet above my head. Even standing on an overturned bucket, I could not reach it, but I thought of the boys alone in the house and I knew if I took too long it would frighten Micah and he would tell his father, again. I did not want to take the time to go back for the ladder. Instead, I climbed on a trash can and onto the gas grill we had brought up from our tiny patio in the city and had stored, along with other odds and ends, in the section of the shed not used for the chickens. My boots were slick with snow, but I felt for traction before putting weight into each step and had a hand on the wall to steady myself. I leaned over the chicken wire partition, connected one plug to the other, and the lamp glowed red. Heat, or at least the idea of heat, washed over me and over my hens, and I felt the satisfaction of having done a good thing. When I dropped one leg down to step back onto the trash can, I moved too quickly and slipped, my boot squeaking against the metal lid.

And this is when I fell.

My back slapped the plywood floor. I opened my mouth to scream but had no breath. I turned my head and retched, then sucked in air, and with the air came an explosive pain in my back. I breathed, trying to control it. I rode the pain like a contraction, but it did not give way, did not break like labor pains.

"Oh!" I cried. My hens shook out their feathers and began to preen. "Oh, oh," I said, again.

I tried to push myself up, to stand, but the pain lit a blaze in my lower back. I could not get up. I could not move.

Now I screamed. I screamed for Micah, for help. I knew it would do no good, my voice could not reach inside the house, or to our nearest neighbor six miles down the road, but I screamed. And then I thought of my phone and patted the coat pockets though I knew it wasn't there, knew it was on the arm of the couch where I had left it, probably dead. We had not hooked up the landline in the house, though there was an old rotary phone still attached to the wall by the microwave. The boys played with it sometimes, Micah calling out "Emergency! Emergency!" into the mouthpiece. It was a toy. There was no one on the other end.

Wind rushed around the corners of the shed. My pain was paralyzing. A dark thing was growing in me, but I tried to push it away. Emergency, I thought. That is what this is.

In the red light, I began to touch myself, to find the source of my pain. My fingers padded around my head, feeling for blood or lumps. I was trying to think logically, to quiet the panic in my chest. My fingertips were numb, though I did not feel cold. When the baby was two months old, he fell off our bed during the night, the thud of his body on the wood floor sickeningly soft, a terrible sound that I felt before I heard. I flew to the floor, holding him to my chest and crying with him, but it was Teddy who turned on the light and laid the baby out, flat, checking his pupils and undressing him to look for bruising.

My neck. My shoulders. My arms. I imagined Teddy over me, saying, *now look here. And here.* I wiped the vomit from my chin with my sleeve. Everything was okay, so far. I worked my way down. The door rattled in the wind and I called out again, thinking maybe, by some miracle, Teddy had come back and was here. But he was not here. He was in Boston. He did not know what I had done.

I felt my way down my body to where the pain centered in my lower back. I pulled up my jacket and touched my belly, and around my hips, and underneath. At first, I thought the rubber handle was part of my body, some odd extremity that had gone numb with my fingers and toes, but as I tried to pull it out from under me the pain flared and when I took my hand away there was blood. The two elements came together in my mind slowly, both the blood and the handle, and I realized I had fallen on a gardening tool, and the tines had gone into the soft area above my pelvis where I knew important organs were located, perhaps kidneys, spleen, intestines. How deep, I couldn't tell, though the claw felt firmly anchored in my flesh. "You've done it, now," I said aloud to myself, and I felt the deranged urge to laugh, though nothing at all was funny.

I'd ordered the claw, and a whole set of gardening implements just after closing on the house. The tools had come nestled in a small wicker basket. The sight filled me with visions of pulling weeds, eating carrots with the greens attached. Collecting strawberries for jam. I wanted all of that. The soil here was stonier than I had expected, though. It was nearly impossible to dig out, or so it seemed. I'd tossed the tools into the shed, where they had been waiting for this very moment to impale me. A claw to the back, as if I were a prey animal freshly caught. Now I did laugh, but it came out a wrenched moan.

Teddy would not let me keep the boys here, after this.

Teddy. His name was Edward but I called him Teddy, his childhood nickname. I used to think it was funny because he bore no resemblance to a teddy bear, but was tall and thin, the kind of man who looked out of place anywhere except in front of a computer. We were married in the courtyard outside town hall, in front of the reflecting pool with its bronze statue of a Minuteman soldier holding a rifle. Many men had died in battle there. Teddy had taken the time to read the plaque. He always took time to read plaques. I loved this about him. He understood facts, how one thing led to another. After Micah was born, I'd been alone in the apartment for hours a day while Teddy was at work, and I had begun to believe ridiculous things, that the apartment was full of lead paint, that it was in the air, that Micah would not be safe unless I cleaned him constantly. It was insane, and I knew that, but I could not stop the thoughts. One day, Teddy came home and I was sitting with Micah in bathwater that had long gone cold, Micah's skin mottling purple. Teddy took two weeks off from work to be home with us, and then arranged for his mother to come by once a day. After that, I did not talk about the lead paint anymore.

Sometimes, when Micah looked at me, I believed he was remembering the way I had been, though he was too good to say it. I believed he saw it in me, still.

The wild wind rose again and now I feared it. I counted my breaths, in and out as one, up to twenty and then I couldn't hold back anymore, and I gulped air too quickly and was dizzy. Something terrible in me, the dark thing that I tried to keep hidden from Teddy, wanted to take off my clothes like those loopy mountaineers in the death zone, to let the cold come quickly to my body, to hasten that easy, drowsy death. I imagined the thickening of blood, the sleepiness coming on like a pill, irresistible. I couldn't shake that dark thing, though I'd tried by moving here to this house, so far away from everything else I had known. I saw that dark thing inside me as a black hole, an emptiness that could not be filled because everything I put into it was obliterated into more emptiness, and I feared it, too. I wondered if it was heritable, if Micah and the baby would have this dark thing in them. And the pain came again, a surge that jolted my spine, as if to say *have you forgotten about me?*

I realized I was shivering when I bit my tongue. I held my jaw tight, tasted blood. Static filled my ears, like a radio out of range. I felt neither warm nor cold, only light, as if I might float up from the floor, and I knew I could fall asleep if I let myself. I was pulling away from my body, and in leaving my body I was leaving that dark thing behind. I was lifting through the roof of the shed and into the storm, and could see our small red house, its flash of color against the white, could picture the boys inside, their warm, beating hearts. And wilderness all around. I saw my children's bodies, the small maps of their arms and legs and foreheads, their symmetries and scents I had dreamed into being. And I was rising, still. The house was growing smaller. Coyotes dotted the landscape, waiting for nightfall. The boys were falling away from me, and the snow was falling, and I was falling, again and again, but up or down, I could not tell.

Without the dark thing, I was unbound. Molecular. I was the storm and I was the wilderness and I was the hungry coyote curling into itself for warmth.

The pain drew me back, hushed at first and then louder and louder, a dial turned up, and again I was on the floor, in my broken body. How I wanted to see my boys. I wanted it fiercely, instinctively, as if there were no other choice. My sons would worry about me. They would grow up to be men who worried, like their father, and this was because of me. It was my doing, leaving them there. If I died here, in the shed, they would certainly die, and that would be my doing, too.

The wind roared again, and I prepared myself, bracing. I rolled onto my good side and tried to pry the claw from my back. I screamed; the pain was too much. The chickens were watching me now, their lizard eyes taking in the spectacle of my suffering, waiting to see if I had the good sense to survive. Perhaps it's better to leave the claw in, I thought, dredging up fragments of the first aid class I took in college. Puncture wounds don't kill you, the blood loss does, or something like that. I would leave it, yes. I would deal with it later when I was inside the house and had towels and hot water.

Without knowing how I would do it, I pushed up to my knees and managed to stand. My back pulsed. I pulled the jacket tight around me, the back moist with blood, and opened the door to the storm, and began to walk into it, dragging the leg on my right side where the claw was, as it would not lift. The hurt part of me seemed to weigh a thousand pounds. What odd tracks I was leaving, an injured beast retreating to its hole. The wind nearly knocked me over, and I leaned into it, focused only on getting back to the house. I did not know what I would do after that—the distance to any hospital would be insurmountable in this weather, and 911 was a joke in these parts—but I could not think of that, now. First, I would get back to my children. I would touch their bodies and know they were safe. Blood was soaking down the back of my pants, and the static was growing louder in my ears, but I was close. I was on the first step, then the second. My hand was on the doorknob.

I opened the door into the kitchen, and called out, expecting them to run to me. There was no answer. I thought the worst, that Micah had gone out into the storm after me, the baby had fallen from the couch, and now all was lost. Again, I called their names. I set my face to hide the pain and kept the jacket around me to cover the claw. My boots were leaving bloody prints on the linoleum. Then, around the corner they came, the two of them, Micah holding a canister of rice puffs and the baby following, his face shiny with tears and mucus. I knelt, slowly, smiling so as not to frighten them.

"He was hungry," Micah said. "I couldn't be a statue anymore." He handed the baby a rice puff and the baby pressed it into his mouth, and they both watched me, warily. They stared, unsure what I was doing there, squatting on the kitchen floor in blood. And I was so elated they were okay, and Micah taking care of his brother. I was so happy I began to sob, and this made them stare more, Micah holding his bangs back from his eyes, and I wanted to explain that I wasn't angry or sad, but this was too much to say, and the pain in my back was growing hot again.

Behind me, a burst of wind threw open the door I had not fully shut. The room began to spin, and I fell onto my knees, the claw ripping more flesh with my movement. It felt real, the claw, as if it were not metal but sinew and bone and keratin, a part of me that had been there all along.

"I'm here, now," I said, which was both the truth and a lie, but my voice was lost to the storm blowing into our house. Snow was gusting into the kitchen. It was mounding by the stove, drifts overtaking the foam mat where I stood to wash dishes. The room was transforming, the inside becoming outside, a beautiful and inhospitable scene like the top of a mountain. I knew I should make it stop, but I was having trouble keeping my eyes open. The oxygen was thinning. I wanted to sleep, to dream through winter and wake, lean and hungry, in the spring. The boys were huddled together, making sounds I could not hear. They were receding. Their downy flesh was prickling at the cold, velvet eyes turned not to me but beyond, through the door, into the wilderness I had called forth.

Remember How I Loved You

Gloria had never been to a hospital like this before. She had been to hospitals to have her babies, c-sections for both girls. She had been in the ER once in college with appendicitis that the triage nurse thought, at first, was a hangover because she threw up on her lap in the waiting room. She had been to a public hospital in Belize on her honeymoon because Phillip had broken his ankle climbing down from their loft bed and it had taken three doctors to figure out how to unfold the wheelchair. There had been other hospitals with her daughters, of course, all of those small emergencies. There was a meningitis scare when Nell was eight, and that time Hannah got into a swarm of hornets when they were hiking Mt. Greylock and her neck swelled up on the way to Berkshire Medical and Gloria had visions of performing a tracheotomy with a pocket knife and a Bic pen right there in the minivan, something she had seen once in a movie, while Phillip drove exactly the speed limit. All of these hospitals were different but alike, all of them with the same antiseptic smell, the fluorescent lights, the understanding that soon you would be made better and sent along your way.

GLORIA WAS FIFTY-THREE NOW, her daughters well past the ages of requiring Band-Aids and kisses on scraped knees, but still Nell had called and asked Gloria to come to this hospital where she had checked herself in. The caller ID showed up on Gloria's phone as BEHAVIORAL MED, which Gloria mistakenly assumed to be the vet calling to let her know the dog's gabapentin prescription was ready, something the behaviorist hoped would stop him from shitting everywhere when he was anxious, but instead, when she answered, Gloria heard Nell's small voice calling out "Mom? Mama?"

"Nellie? What's going on?" Gloria had said, so loudly the dog jumped up from his place at her feet and farted audibly.

In the background, Gloria could make out a television and other people's voices, and Gloria wondered if Nell was in a waiting room, somewhere, like the lobby of a Jiffy Lube. Gloria used to tell Phillip to check Nell's Camry when she came for dinner because it was something Gloria's own father had done for her, "let me take a peek at those fluids" he'd always said, though what fluids, Gloria had no idea, and apparently Phillip didn't either because his idea of checking the car was to run a finger along the tire treads and mutter to himself.

"Is something wrong with your car?" Gloria asked.

"Mom," Nell said. "I need you to promise you won't freak out."

It was a kind of code in their family, prefacing bad news this way. Just those words could split a room into before and after. Two years ago, Phillip had used those words before telling Gloria he'd fallen in love with the paraprofessional aid in his class, a girl just out of college, and was asking for a divorce.

When Nell spoke again her voice was quick and flat, as if she were reading from a script. She proceeded to tell Gloria that she had been going through a hard time since switching to fully remote work, that she was struggling with her mental health, and she was having a depressive episode—that's how she put it, *a depressive episode*, as if it were a television show in which she'd been unwittingly cast—and she was taking some time for herself. In a hospital. Gloria could tell she had repeated this story many times before, out loud to doctors and nurses, and probably in her head, too, getting her story straight in the way that she did, this girl whose life had never before strayed from its path: an English degree from Wellesley, editorial work in Boston, her own apartment, tap dancing lessons for adults at the conservatory. Even as a child, Nell always seemed to know what she wanted, and Gloria, who had never quite figured that out for herself, had trusted Nell's judgment in just about everything, whether she understood it or not. It didn't help that Nell was a good head taller than Gloria, with a cup size Gloria hadn't achieved even while lactating. She saw none of her genes in the girl. Gloria had sometimes joked—not seriously, of course, but with a hint of truth—that she had brought the wrong baby home from the hospital, and somewhere out there a bewildered Scandinavian family was wondering how they'd ended up with such an indecisive, frizzy-haired daughter.

Gloria sat on the edge of the couch, her mouth, like the dog's, open and panting. "Oh honey," she said. "I don't understand. You're doing so well!" It was Hannah they worried about, not Nell. Wasn't it just last month that Gloria had helped Nell pick out new glass doors for her landlord to install in her shower? Gloria liked them so much she'd texted the listing to Phillip, trying to establish that coparenting link he claimed to want, though her text only showed delivered and not read.

"Mom, please," Nell said. "People are waiting for the phone. Just come."

GLORIA'S ENTRY TO Pember Point Behavioral Hospital required being buzzed through two sets of thick doors. In the lobby, faint steel drum music played and the air smelled like a Yankee candle had been burning for too long. As she tried to orient herself, a male nurse in lavender scrubs pointed a thermometer at her forehead, nodded, and told her to place her jacket and purse into a complimentary locker. The word "BREATHE," spelled out in polished driftwood, hung on the shiplapped wall behind the front desk.

"The shoes, too, ma'am," he added, glancing at the worn New Balance sneakers Gloria favored because they accommodated her worsening bunions.

It was visiting hour, and there were other people around Gloria, tottering to pull off boots, shoving winter coats into lockers, a bunch of strangers standing around in their stocking feet. For a moment, Gloria stood, unmoving, wondering if all of this was one big mistake, perhaps her car's GPS had brought her to the wrong location, like the time she ended up in a synagogue parking lot instead of the UPS Store, and she felt the familiar, dizzying sense of having been plopped down into a life that did not belong to her. The past two years since Phillip left had been like a strange dream, each morning she wished to wake up to her old, wonderful life—Phillip riding the bike in the guest room, the girls sharing an iPad on the couch, watching YouTube or taking pictures of each other with silly filters—and now she was here, in this unlikely place. She wanted to leave, to run back through those doors to her car and then, where, back to her empty house? Gloria pictured the single-serve chopped Caesar salad she would end up eating for dinner, the dog's begging head on her lap while she swiped through her matches on Golden Singles, and the last bit of hope dissolved in her churning stomach.

The nurse led them down a hallway into an exercise room with treadmills and rowing machines and stacks of rainbow-colored gymnastic pads, all seemingly brand new. The room looked as if it belonged in a college brochure rather than a psychiatric hospital and Gloria wondered how much all of this was costing, though that hardly mattered now, and anyway she was glad Nell wasn't just lying on a white bed in a white room, staring listlessly. Gloria watched as the other visitors claimed balance balls and sat cross-legged on yoga mats, and she chose a weight bench in the corner and sat tentatively on the side with the leg extension, nervous the split bench might flip up if she put her weight on it wrong. She was wearing the fuzzy Grinch socks Hannah had given them all for Christmas, which she wouldn't have worn if she'd known about the shoes rule, and catching sight of them, she crossed her ankles under the bench. Breathe, she told herself, as the driftwood had instructed.

And then, the patients came in, all in some version of pajama pants and T-shirts, dazed expressions on their faces. The nurse positioned himself in the doorway, hands behind his back. "Twenty minutes, folks," he said.

Nell was in a Black Dog shirt Gloria recognized from their family trip several summers back, before the divorce, when both girls were finally brave enough to jump off the Jaws bridge and Phillip had gotten sick from food truck clams. Nell's blond hair looked unbrushed and greasy, and one side of her forehead was broken out in tiny pimples. It was almost too much for Gloria, seeing her usually Instagram-ready daughter like this, and in order not to appear upset she pressed her face into the same overly enthusiastic smile she used when her friends asked, "but how are you *really?*" She stood, opening her arms as Nell approached, and Nell, eyes down, stopped short of walking into Gloria's hug but permitted herself to be held. Nell's body towered over her, and Gloria felt, as she had since Nell was an adolescent, that she was the child and Nell the grown-up, but Gloria held her nonetheless, reassuring herself with Nell's familiar flesh and her slightly tangy scent that always reminded Gloria of fresh bread.

"It's okay, Mom," Nell said, stepping back.

Nell's bottom lip was split and covered in chapped flakes and her face had, seemingly overnight, developed the sunken marionette lines on her cheeks that made her seem older than twenty-six.

"You look tired," Gloria said before she could stop herself.

Nell blinked at the words. They sat. Nell fidgeted on the bench, making the legs creak. Around them, people began to talk or laugh or fight. One patient, a woman with short, tufted hair, was crying like a child, her mouth wide open. Gloria leaned toward Nell, resisting the urge to push Nell's hair away from her face and tell her she did not belong here. Nell had been the happiest toddler, every moment a delight, a girl who would shriek with glee because Gloria held her up to press the garage door opener. Where had all that happiness gone? How could it simply vanish?

"Are they feeding you?" Gloria asked, instead.

"Yes, Mom, of course."

"You have to eat," Gloria continued. She had this problem of saying the wrong thing and then doubling down on it. Phillip's word was *perseverate*. The sixth grade class Phillip taught included kids with autism, and when they perseverated by asking the same question over and over, Phillip told them "I am not going to talk about this anymore," and then he wouldn't. He'd considered it a superpower, this ability to tune things out, including Gloria when she went on too much about one hypothetical worry or another. Gloria liked to picture him doing the same with his new girlfriend, letting her prattle while he calmly turned the pages of his book.

"Mom," Nell said.

"I've been so worried, Nellie! Hannah is worried, too." She paused, then added "And Daddy."

Gloria could tell she'd said the wrong thing again, admitting that she'd already told the rest of the family. Nell pulled one long leg up to her chest and pressed her chin to her knee. Her grippy-socked toes folded over the edge of the bench. Her fingernails were painted with the mauve polish Nell had wanted for Christmas that Gloria thought was an odd color—Dusty Pearl—something Gloria's grandmother might have worn, but on Nell, as always, it had been lovely. Gloria felt suddenly pleased that at least her daughter had this, these pretty, polished fingernails that looked freshly done. Clearly, she had taken the time to do several coats, to make sure to get all the way to the edges, her brush strokes smooth and exact. She had cared enough to do that.

Nell placed her cheek against her thigh and closed her eyes as if in some kind of discomfort. "How is Hannah, anyway?" she asked.

"Oh, she's alright," Gloria said. It seemed odd talking about Hannah with Nell in such a state, but she followed Nell's lead. "Did she tell you her history professor agreed to let her make up the mid-term?"

"Oh," Nell said. "She better study this time."

Gloria laughed a little, which felt wrong, under the circumstances, but then Nell laughed too, and she opened her eyes and sniffed.

"She'll figure it out," Gloria said, though she wasn't sure if that was true. There was momentum to the way life unraveled; one bad thing invited another, and who was to say where it ended? Gloria wished she could protect her daughters as she had when they were small enough to fit into a carrier strapped to her chest. How she'd once envied those animals who were built for that type of thing, the marsupials with their pouches, the crocodiles who could carry their young in their mouths, the frogs who could swallow down their eggs and belch their children out, fully formed.

"If you need to come home for a while," Gloria began.

"I don't." Nell squinted at her leg, as if consulting an invisible plan. "I mean, I'm working through it. That's why I'm here."

"How long will you stay?" Gloria asked. How much time did it take to work through things?

"I have two weeks sick-leave," Nell said. She straightened up, then slumped forward again. "So, two weeks, I guess."

Nell was a rule follower like her father, though once he'd broken that first rule with the affair, all bets were off. For weeks after he moved out, Gloria had waited for Phillip's car to pull into the driveway, convinced the gravitational pull of their life together would be inescapable. Their marriage had been no different than other marriages, Gloria had thought, imperfect and stale, maybe, but too big a part of each of them to be easily shed. In this she had been wrong.

The voices in the room rose and fell and Gloria searched for what to say, the question that would illuminate the source of Nell's pain without revealing her own, but it was becoming harder and harder for Gloria to separate the two. Should she suggest Nell ask to have her old job back at Macmillan where she had gotten along so well with everyone? Surely remote work wasn't her only option, not at her age. Or maybe Nell could try another tap dancing retreat like the one she'd gone to last summer in Charlotte; she'd come back so excited about learning that Maxi Ford move and had spent over $100 on replacement screws and cleaning for her tap shoes.

Or was there more to her daughter's depression? Had Gloria's loneliness rubbed off on Nell? Was it contagious? Was it because Nell's landlord had ended up installing the wrong shower doors? Nell had called Gloria crying when she found they were opaque rather than clear, and Gloria had tried her best to commiserate, though it seemed like such a small thing at the time. Could the worry of soap scum build-up push someone into a depressive episode? She wished it could be simple like it was, once, when Gloria had the magic to make Nell's eyes light up by giving her quarters for the merry-go-round outside Market Basket. Her parenting skills had not really evolved much past that point, and she felt just as powerless to fix her daughters' lives as she was to fix her own.

"What can I do?" Gloria asked.

In the treadmill section, a man stood and began slapping himself on the forehead.

"Just keep talking," Nell said, softly.

So, Gloria did. She talked about Hannah for a while, just the same old things like the butterfly tattoo on Hannah's right earlobe that Gloria worried would prevent anyone from ever taking her seriously, and then about Nell's best friend from high school whom Gloria had seen on Facebook, getting her ESL certification and moving to South Korea, and Nell said she'd heard it was really nice there, even though the rain was so acidic you had to carry an umbrella with you, and they went back and forth on this, wondering if such a thing could be true, and what would happen if you got caught in the rain without protection. Would it turn your hair green? And they remembered the time Nell's hair had turned green from the pool at the Y, and Gloria had tried stripping it with baking soda and it turned into one big snarl and she'd had to cut most of it off. They remembered other things, too, moments that had been bad at the time but now felt close to joy, like when they all got seasick on a snorkeling cruise in Puerto Rico, and when they'd had to wait so long for an airport shuttle outside Logan that little Hannah peed her pants.

Gloria wanted to go on and on remembering, but the nurse gave them a five minute warning. The reverie was broken. Nell ran her hands through her hair. "Have you been on any more dates?" she asked, snapping Gloria back to the present. Gloria's last Golden Singles date was with a paunchy DPW worker and had ended with Gloria paying the check and waiting awkwardly outside the restaurant in the rain for her date's mother to show up to drive him home.

"No," she said, leaving it at that. Nell shrugged and told her she had to keep at it, which was what everyone said. Press onward, don't give up! But why? Gloria did not ask.

The years when the girls were young had been the happiest of Gloria's life, their small, warm bodies like goodness made flesh, and Gloria had somehow thought life would be like that forever, though it had passed in a flash. Phillip understood; he'd been quick to find new pleasures. Sometimes the house was so empty it made Gloria feel that nothing would ever be truly good again, that those years of being so furiously loved had ruined her for this solitary life, and perhaps this was part of what Nell was going through, too. Maybe those years ruin us all, Gloria thought. Children hardened into adults, and parents turned back into their lonely, flawed, unmagical selves, and this was an unstoppable part of life. What this hospital could do to make that feeling go away for her daughter, Gloria could not imagine, but she hoped very much that it could.

When the visiting session was over, Nell stood and looked toward the door where the other patients were lining up, her face resolute. "It's time for group meditation," she said.

"I'll come back tomorrow," Gloria said. She held Nell's cheeks and Nell bent down so Gloria could kiss the uninflamed side of her forehead. She closed her eyes and pressed her lips against her daughter's skin.

"I'll be here," Nell said.

AT HOME, GLORIA LET HERSELF into the unlit kitchen. It was barely 4:30 but the sun was nearly gone. She had turned down the thermostat before leaving and now the air bit her nostrils, along with the acrid scent of fresh shit. The dog whined at her feet, his claws clicking on the hardwood. The smell of feces surrounded her. It was probably ground into the rug, again. The dog went flat on his belly, tail sweeping the floor, repentant.

Gloria opened the cabinet under the sink and took out plastic gloves and the red bottle of cleaner and a brush. She found the shit in the hallway, smeared into the runner as well as the baseboard on one side. As she scrubbed, the dog sniffed inquisitively at his own mess, as if he'd already forgotten what he'd done, which likely he had, though when he realized what it was, he grew bored and left Gloria to do her work, alone. Even with her scrubbing, the runner would retain that off smell. After the next time, she would roll it up and throw it into the trash bin.

When she was done, Gloria brought the brush to the sink and washed her hands. Soon, she would make her salad and eat it under a blanket on the couch, and then she would call Phillip with an update on Nell. She was already thinking of how she could draw out the conversation by asking him about the new house and how Dierdre was doing with her graduate work. Even though it would grate, it would still comfort her to hear the voice she had heard for so many years of her life.

And after that, perhaps she would call Hannah to see if she wanted to come home from school this weekend. They could visit Nell and then go out to dinner at that Indian place Hannah liked so much, and afterwards Gloria would take her to TJ Maxx and let her pick out whatever she wanted, whatever caught her eye. She would watch Hannah flit through the store, flipping through the racks while bopping along to a playlist streaming in the one earbud that seemed permanently embedded in her tattooed ear, and she would follow along, absorbing every bit of it. She would soak up the moment, hoarding it for later. "Are you happy?" Gloria might ask, as they left the store, bags in hand, and Hannah would laugh and say "Yeah, sure, Mom. Are you?"

Or maybe she would not ask. Maybe it was enough to hope for it. Maybe Nell would get better and be discharged early and Hannah would graduate from college and become a marine biologist like she always wanted, studying the language of orcas. Maybe the dog would stop having accidents. Maybe Gloria would learn how to get through this stage of life, she would figure out the right things to say and when to say them, and she would go on dates with men who owned their own vehicles and asked questions about her and listened when she answered. She would brag to them about her beautiful girls, and they would nod and agree that yes, Gloria was very lucky. Not everyone had such blessings. There were some people who never knew real happiness in life. There were some people who never knew what it was to be loved at all.

Distance

Lena is twenty-nine when her father asks her to run the Boston Marathon with him. "It's a dream of mine," he has written on printer paper and sent through the actual mail. "Think about it. We'd make a great team."

His cursive script is wiry, as his body was the last time she had been to the farm, two years ago. In the photo her father includes with his letter he is still thin, but not sunken-cheeked like when he and Lena's mother were married. His girlfriend, Storm, has taken it. On the back he writes "Dad, harvesting first crop of husk cherries," as if Lena wouldn't recognize his curly hair, graying now, or the three-acre plot of soil in the background where her childhood sustenance had been grown. As if she could forget those long Maine winters eating frozen zucchini, canned beets, carrots and potatoes stored in five-gallon buckets in the cellar.

Via text, Lena agrees. Since college, she has lived in Newton, Massachusetts, crossing over the marathon route on Commonwealth Avenue on her drive to work at the library, and she knows the marathon is in April, eight months away. In that time, she can lose the weight she's gained since Finny moved in, maybe more. Or, alternately, her father may move onto some new fitness fad, like glacier hiking, or barefoot trail running, and forget about the marathon. Either way. Maybe she doesn't take him too seriously, this man who comes and goes in her life according to a pattern she has never been able to discern.

Lena calls her mother, forgetting she has gone to San Juan for the week. Straining to make herself heard over thumping music on her mother's end, Lena explains the marathon plans and receives a warning that she knows too well: "Your father is a very serious person." Growing up, in the time before Lena and her mother left the farm and moved into the duplex on Green Street, Lena was often afraid to ask her father to sign a field-trip permission slip or to drive her to a friend's house for sledding and hot cocoa, because these were the kinds of things that could set him off—not in anger, but in profound, existential concern. "McDonald's is poison," he might say. Or "I need you to remember what Nestlé has done in underdeveloped countries." Lena's mother had made the mistake of not taking him too seriously, herself, in her younger days. "I thought he looked like James Taylor," she used to say, clicking her tongue. "Those curls."

"He's different now. The farm has Wi-Fi!" Lena shouts into the phone. She doesn't add that she knows this because she has watched Storm's yoga videos on YouTube, has seen the second-floor bedroom where she once slept turned into a brightly lit, sleekly modern studio.

Lena's mother does not respond for a moment, long enough for Lena to wonder if she should repeat herself, louder. The salsa beat vibrates between them and Lena pictures her mother dancing, throwing her hips around in a way Lena never would. "Okay, honey," Lena's mother says, finally, in a tone that tells Lena the conversation is over. "It's your life."

Saturday morning, Lena's alarm goes off, and she gets out of bed while Finny continues to snore gently on his back. In the kitchen, she fills a glass with warm tap water and adds a splash of apple cider vinegar from a nearly empty bottle in the back of the cupboard, a mixture she remembers her father swearing by to activate detoxification and ward off stiffness. She finds Storm's Sun Salutation workout—her channel is called Purple Lotus and has a surprising amount of subscribers—and plays it on her phone on mute. She doesn't have a mat, and grit from the linoleum floor sticks to her palms. She layers two pairs of Finny's tube socks, her father's trick to avoid blisters, and pulls the scrunched-up paper from inside the sneakers she had bought last spring, still in their Amazon box. She stretches her calves against the wall, and then she opens the door and begins to run.

Outside, the cold air is a knife in her chest. Her thighs chafe, and after two blocks, her diaphragm cramps and her gait becomes a shuffle. She's panting, vinegar bubbling up into her throat. Passing the glassy side of Whole Foods, she sees her huffing, jiggling self reflected, and though she quickly turns away, the energy has gone out of her. She walks home, heels burning, and when she comes through the door she meets Finny, bundled in his wool sweater with a Red Bull in one hand, heading to the porch for his morning smoke. He stumbles to avoid colliding with her. "Whoa, babe," he says.

She tries again Sunday, waiting until the air has warmed. She pushes herself close to a mile, and for a couple blocks she hits a stride and begins to lose sense of her body as something separate from the motion. Her scalp tingles with endorphins. She refuses to acknowledge her reflection in the storefronts. She thinks about the text she will send her father, reporting her training, writing it one way and then another in her head.

When she gets back to the apartment, Finny is lying on the couch with his phone, a box of Pop-Tarts on the floor. She pushes his feet aside to sit on the edge of the cushion, and takes her time untying her shoes, waiting for him to notice she is there and to say something about her sudden change of habit, but he pulls his feet from behind her and presses his toes into the crack between cushions, scrolling to the next video. He is younger than Lena by six years, something she keeps from her friends, most of whom are married. When they met, Finny was working at Neighborhood Bakery across from the library, but he overslept too many times and was fired. He has the most beautiful face she's ever seen on a man, full lips and green eyes with feathery lashes, and he has never once said a cruel word to Lena, though conversation is not a significant component of their relationship. Mostly they get high and order food and watch low budget sci-fi movies that Finny rents on Lena's Prime account. She is not sure how she feels about him, and he doesn't ask much anymore. Some nights, when she goes to bed after him, he lifts the covers as she crawls in, something no other man has ever done for her.

"Hungry?" she asks, because she is. She likes it when Finny gets IHOP delivered, even though the pancakes are always cold.

"What? No, I'm good," he says, reaching down for the Pop-Tarts and handing her the box. She holds it for a moment, smelling the fake strawberry goodness, then sets it on the floor.

In the kitchen, Lena tries to find something healthy in the fridge. Her father once consumed five pounds of vegetables each day, most of them whole, though for a few years before he took them off grid she remembers him using an electric juicer for the beets and peppers and then, because he refused to waste it, cooking off the leftover pulp in a giant stock pot on the stove. The mixture would sit there for days, smelling like compost, nobody but her father daring to eat it. Lena looks through the vegetable drawer, takes out baby carrots that have gone white and shriveled in their bag. She's been able to do it before, to eat like her father, to starve away excess. In college, sophomore year, she could count each rib below her breasts. She'd watched her hip bones turn to knobs, her cheeks grow taut and creased in parentheses around her mouth, just like his. It had felt freeing to Lena, as if in her lightness she could slip the constraints of physics, could lift higher with each step, could melt into air, and she imagined that is what her father felt, as well, though she had no way of knowing. Eventually, a professor expressed concern over her transformation and referred her to the mental health services on campus. Ashamed, Lena ate every Snickers in the dorm vending machine, one after another, balling up the wrappers and pressing them under her mattress. When the weight returned, her friends said she looked so much more like herself.

Lena bites the tip of a carrot and then puts the whole thing in her mouth. It tastes of nothing, mashing to fibrous shreds between her teeth, but she forces it down and throws the rest of the bag into the trash. On her phone, she finds her father's contact and types "first training day in the books," adding a cute sneaker emoji. She hits send and waits. She taps her phone to keep it lit, hoping to see the dot dot dot that means he is writing back. She considers sending another text reporting her distance but hesitates. There have been whole years in Lena's life in which she and her father have not communicated beyond the happy birthday email he always sends, two days late, and the Christmas card she always sends, which he has never mentioned, and now that he is back in her life in a real way, Lena is nervous she will do something to ruin it. After several minutes of no reply, Lena puts the phone down. She goes back to the couch. The Pop-Tarts are where she left them. She leans close to Finny as she opens a shiny foil package. He puts a sweatered arm around her. If he notices crumbs falling on his legs, he doesn't complain.

Through the fall and into the winter, Lena runs. Her father emails every few weeks with an update of his daily distance and regimen, and she writes back with her mileage and how much weight she is losing. He is pleased. "Terrific work," he says. Lena feels as though she is making up for those years after the divorce, when her father was alone on the farm and her mother would not allow visitation. He obtains sponsorship by Dana Farber so they can enter the marathon without pre-qualifying, since Lena has not run a marathon before. He says it doesn't matter if they start the race in the front with the qualifiers, or in the back with the others, though he did achieve a qualifying time at the Maine Marathon in Portland.

During these months, Lena cooks meals of steamed broccoli and rice, cubed tofu, watery soups with farro and kale, recipes that remind her of father's "Diet for a Small Planet" cookbook that she finds on Pinterest. She drinks water from canning jars. In moments of weakness, she sucks the candy coating off of M&Ms and spits the chocolate out. She stops sharing Finny's peanut butter pretzels and Chex Mix at night when they watch movies, and then she stops watching movies, choosing to sleep because she knows when her alarm goes off at 5:00 a.m., she must run. Finny doesn't ask questions; his lovely face registers no distress that Lena can discern, though she looks for it. When she gets up in the mornings, she often finds him asleep on the couch, using his sweater as a blanket. One morning, he isn't there, and Lena doesn't text or call him, though she does check his location on her phone throughout the day and is relieved he is always at his mother's house. He returns two days later, carrying a Stop & Shop bag full of chips and cereal and an iced coffee, and they both act as if nothing has changed.

Christmas comes. Lena's mother goes to Paris. Lena and Finny walk through Newton Highlands, sharing a joint and a Styrofoam cup of coffee, stopping at Crystal Lake to sit on a bench and stare at the frozen water. Lena thinks of the past August when she and Finny went night swimming in their underwear, how Finny had held her in the water, her legs wrapped around him, while they quietly had sex, hidden from passing cars in the L of the dock. He told her he loved her that night, and the words had felt warm on her wet neck, though she could not say them back. She wonders if Finny is thinking of this, too, and she turns to him, looking for that flicker of memory, but his eyes are flat as he inhales in his practiced way, then exhales politely to the side. He hands her the stub of joint. "Think it's cashed," he says.

The next day, Lena drives to Maine, to the farm. Her father stands in the door as she parks in front of the barn. Getting out of her car, the air bites her nostrils, her breath turning to vapor. Lena cannot hold back her smile as she walks toward her father, and her father smiles, too, his hand lifting in hello. He is wearing jeans and moccasins and a thin V-neck sweater with nothing underneath, his hair back in a low ponytail, and he looks exactly the way Lena remembers him, exactly like himself, and warmth surges in Lena's chest. At the door, she pauses, grinning, unsure if she should hug him. He reaches for her and she begins to lean in, but his hand lands on her overnight bag, and he takes it from her and moves back into the house. "Come on. Don't let the cold in," he says.

Inside, the kitchen is dim and smells of clove. Lena takes off her jacket and hangs it on a peg by the wood stove, as she once did as a child, and her father sets her bag on the table and pours tea from a kettle into two mugs, handing one to her. "You look good," he says.

Lena nods, pleased. "Thanks," she says. She looks around the kitchen, takes in the wide planked floors, the horsehair plaster walls, the cast iron sink where she once was made to wash her hair with water boiled over the fire. Now there's LED lights under the cabinets and a Bluetooth speaker on the windowsill, and what appears to be brand name paper towels by the ceramic canister that holds spatulas and wooden spoons. She takes a sip of her tea, a strong cinnamon, the heat sinking into her. "I brought my running shoes," she says. Her father raises his mug and they softly clink cheers.

"To the marathon," he says.

"To the marathon," she says.

They run the loop of road that takes them from the farm to a short stretch of Route 1, then back onto narrow gravel roads that for most of Lena's childhood were named only by numbers. The afternoon sun is crystalline against the snow. Their pace is unrushed, and Lena carefully matches her stride to her father's, not wanting to go too fast or too slow. He watches her form and makes corrections, telling her to let her hands hang loose by her hips, to push forward rather than up, and Lena does. At one point, a fox trots across the road in front of them and disappears into the trees, and Lena and her father turn to each other with wide, ecstatic eyes. They do not say a word. Perhaps they do not need to speak, she thinks. Perhaps they are communicating through their footfalls and breaths and the way they run side by side at the edge of the road, her father between her and where the oncoming traffic would be, if there were any. Perhaps, she thinks, this is what it is to be known.

After, while they cool down, they walk the perimeter of the farm, Lena's father pointing out the new solar panels on the barn and the rock sculptures Storm—who, he adds with no sign of bitterness, has decided to winter in Brazil, solo—had created around the garden, which are supposed to bring blessings of plenitude. At night, they eat soup and warm bread in the kitchen, their meal lit only by the glowing LED lights, listening to Cat Stevens on Bluetooth, and her father does not ask why Lena eats only the broth and small pinches of bread. Lena feels more at home than she ever remembers feeling, even when the farm was her home.

When they finish, Lena helps her father with the dishes, watching him fill one side of the sink with soapy water and the other with rinsing water as he has always done, the only person Lena knows who washes dishes without running the tap the whole time. His ponytail is coming loose, and he is humming along with the music, and Lena has the overwhelming urge to tell him things about her life, about the library and Finny and about the dull ache of hunger that she is always trying so hard to ignore. She wants to ask him what it means to be alone, and if he is sad about Storm. She wants him to tell her everything is okay, and that everything about her is okay, even the things that aren't.

"Maybe we can run again tomorrow," she says.

Her father drops a ladle into the rinse water and Lena fishes it out and places it onto the drying rack. "I plan to," he says.

The kitchen is warm and dim and Cat Stevens is singing mournfully about trouble, and Lena thinks it is beautiful, and her father is beautiful, and she yearns to be part of it, to be beautiful, too. "I could stay another night," she says, putting the idea out there. "I mean, I've got the time off work."

He waits for the song to finish before responding. "They don't need you at the cafe?"

Lena realizes he is referring to her last job at Panera. He'd never been to one and didn't realize it was a chain, which was probably for the best. She hasn't worked there in four years. Surely her father knows this.

"No," she says. The rinse water is growing cold. Lena looks at her hands resting on the edge of the sink. The space between them seems to have widened, though neither of them has moved. "I work at the library now. I'm the head of circulation."

Her father takes in this information while scouring the Dutch oven with steel wool. Lena can smell the rusty metal. "Well," he says. "Very good, then. A library. You always did like to read."

Lena pictures the Newton Free Library, the massive brick building, the hundreds of patrons that come through its doors each day. Growing up, her father didn't like the idea of library cards, the way they kept track. She is certain he has no idea what she does at her job, as it has very little to do with reading. "Anyway," she says. A shrug.

Her father hands her the Dutch oven and she lowers it into the water. He wipes his hands on his shirt and presses them against his lower back, arching back with a puff of air through his lips. His face is serious, showing no emotion. "You can stay as long as you want, of course. Of course you can. Just keep an eye on the weather."

What he means, Lena assumes, is don't let yourself get snowed in here. Stay, but not too long. It is the answer she should have expected. Lena lifts the Dutch oven from the rinse water and sets it back on top of the stove. She tears a paper towel to dry her hands.

Her father puts up a finger, stopping her. He opens a drawer and hands her a rag, and takes the half-used paper towel from her, laying it flat on the counter to dry.

"Right," Lena says. She is immediately shaken by a sense of embarrassment, though she isn't sure if it's because she's forgotten about her father's rule of rationing paper goods, or because her father is drying a used paper towel so he can add it back to the roll. "Sorry," she says.

IN THE MORNING, LENA WAKES before dawn but her father is already up and outside, shifting firewood from the side of the barn to the stack under the eaves of the house near the front door. She packs her bag and downs a cup of tea with little ceremony, watching through the kitchen window as her father performs his task in his brown L.L.Bean canvas jacket, the only coat Lena has ever known him to own. As she is preparing to leave, her father knocks his boots on the front step and enters the house, a bundle of wood under each arm. "Oh," he says, seeing her with her own jacket on, bag on her shoulder.

"Bye, Dad," Lena says. She has made up her mind to hug him, and she does, quickly, throwing her arms around his neck and pressing her cheek to the cold zipper on his chest.

"Oh," he says again, hefting the firewood up over his hips, held to the spot by Lena's body. "Alright, then." On the drive back, Lena stops at the first gas station she passes and gets a party-sized bag of Doritos which she eats, licking her fingers clean, all the way to Newton.

EARLY SPRING, FINNY GOES to his mother's house and doesn't come back. Lena tracks him on her phone for a few days and finally decides to text him, twice, asking what's up and when is he coming home, but he doesn't respond. What remains is his stash of food in the cupboard above the microwave, along with a barely used toothbrush Lena set out for him by the bathroom sink months ago. Knowing he is gone, the apartment feels altered, though little has actually changed. Her kettlebells and yoga mat still clutter the living room; her clumps of beets and Swiss chard from Whole Foods continue to fill the refrigerator and spill out onto the counter. In the bedroom, Lena's running clothes are scattered across the bed, hung over the mirror, piled onto the scale on the floor. Her books cover the nightstand. She cannot remember the last time Finny's side of the bed was unmade.

A week goes by. Lena thinks of her father, the way they ran together at Christmas, that feeling of connection, and she misses him. For several days she debates writing him a letter and sending it through the mail, confessing her worries, her fears that this loneliness is a permanent defect of her genetic make-up. Instead, she decides a text is better. "I have the apartment to myself, now," she types, adding a smiling emoji in the place of punctuation, omitting the reality that what she did not have, anymore, was a boyfriend, or friend, or whatever Finny was. "Why don't you come down the day before the marathon and stay with me?" She envisions the two of them making a whole wheat spaghetti dinner, threading new laces through their sneakers and strategizing for Heartbreak Hill, and the image feels hopeful, but not impossible. Her father will understand how it feels to find yourself suddenly abandoned, and she wants to believe he can sense the loneliness in her, and, somehow, make it go away.

She waits for her father's reply while simultaneously trying not to think about it. On her fifteen-minute breaks from the circulation desk, she checks her phone, but not while she is at the desk, or stopped at red lights, or in between yoga workouts. She tries to imagine her father inside her apartment and worries what he will think of her stupidly large television, her unfiltered tap water. She worries the traffic noise will keep him awake. She wonders if she should reassure him the farm will be fine without him, that spending the night with her in the city will not disrupt his circadian rhythm. Each day, coming home to her silent apartment, she feels uneasy. In the mornings, instead of running, she sleeps until her alarm goes off four times, and at night, curling into the arm of the couch, she consumes the food Finny left behind, first the Oreos and Pop-Tarts and then the chips, leaving just enough remaining in each package so there will be something for Finny, if he comes back.

When she hears her father's text ding boldly on her phone, she is relieved, but as she taps it open her chest tightens. The text is surprisingly long, and Lena imagines him slowly tapping out the letters with the callused pads of his thumbs, careful to get the words right. He writes that he is doing work in the pine grove, thinning out the trees diseased with blister rust. He adds that Storm might be flying back from Rio soon. "Don't think it would be a good idea," is all he says about her invitation. "Keep training." Quickly, she swipes left to delete the message. After that, she doesn't run again.

ON RACE DAY, THE WEATHER is overcast and cool. Showers are predicted. In Maine, Lena's father wakes up at 4:00 a.m. and drives four and a half hours south on I-95 to her apartment. She waits for him outside, standing alone in the parking lot. When he pulls up, he leans across the seat to push open her door, and his eyes lock, unapologetically, on her body. She is eighteen pounds heavier than she was at Christmas. In shorts, her thighs dimple against the car seat. She doesn't have to tell her father she hasn't trained in two months, that she has allowed herself to resume eating and behaving like herself again, that every pound she has gained makes her feel both guilty and vindicated because it means that she is not like her father, that they are not the same, that she will not end up like him. Her father does not look at her for long.

The rain begins while they are waiting with their corral of runners, charity marathon bibs pinned to the fronts of their shirts. They are in wave three, starting at 10:50 a.m. Around them, people shoot looks at the sky.

"Good," Lena's father says. He squares his shoulders. "Rain gives us an advantage. Nobody likes the rain, but it keeps you from overheating. You're wearing double socks, right?"

"Yes," Lena answers. She wants to go home. "It's cold," she says.

"You won't feel it."

"I don't know."

Her father's face shows no emotion, only a flickering, animal-like alertness, his gaze darting across the crowds. "There's nothing to know. You're going to do your best." Dampened strands of hair pull free from his ponytail and fall into his eyes.

The runners in front of them start to move and the pack opens up, and they begin to jog.

"Keep it even," her father says. Other runners surge past, kicking up water. "Let them go," he says. "We'll find our pace."

Lena keeps her stride short and her arms loose. She focuses on not bouncing, and pushing forward from the balls of her feet. Her father stays at her side, chin raised. His breath goes in and out in measured puffs. Lena breathes through her mouth. Though her face is wet with rain, her lips grow dry and tight, sticking to her teeth.

"Eyes up," her father says. "Shake out those fists."

A mile on, Lena's diaphragm cramps. The stitch throbs with each footfall. She holds her stomach.

"You've got to cough it out, like this," her father says. He makes a deep retching sound, bending himself in half on the exhale.

"Dad," Lena says, looking behind to see if anyone has seen him.

"Come on," he says. Again, he bends and retches. Lena feels herself leaving her body, visualizes her couch, the burrow of her apartment.

"I just need to walk a minute," she says.

"Walk?" Her father shakes his head like a dog after a swim, clearing the hair from his eyes. "No, Lena," he says.

Lena takes a deep inhale, and then coughs and doubles over, closing her eyes for a moment so as not to see people staring. She coughs so hard she nearly gags, feeling close to vomiting. But her father is right. The stitch loosens.

After the eight-mile marker Lena gets another cramp, this one in her hamstring. She jogs with a limp, then slows to a walk. Her father looks at her, alarmed, hair frizzing around his face.

"What is it?" he asks. "Need a bathroom break?"

Lena shakes her head. "I can't do it."

"That's nonsense," he says. He is jogging in place. Groups of people run around them, sodden sneakers smacking the pavement. Her father watches her, confused, his forehead wrinkling. "We're almost halfway."

Lena rubs the back of her thigh, though it doesn't really hurt as much as she wants it to. She is wet and cold. She wants to go back to her apartment and take a hot shower and eat pizza in her bathrobe. She didn't expect to make it this far, and she knows she does not have any more miles in her. "I can't," she says, again, meaning the marathon, the endurance and sacrifice of it, but also what she means is "I can't be like you." She braces for the argument to come. Rain drops thicken and break on the road.

Her father smooths a hand over his hair. "Are you sure?" His eyes meet Lena's and she sees he is not angry. He is not disappointed. He is just serious.

"I'll look for you at the finish line," she says, and then turns away, pushes through the onlookers, and climbs a slick grassy embankment. She imagines her father standing, staring at her back, disbelieving, waiting for her to change her mind and return to him and the race. But when she looks back to urge him on, he is not there. He has pulled ahead, keeping pace with a new group of racers. Still, Lena waves at the spot where he had been, at the straggling runners, drenched in the cold rain, doing their best to believe that the end is not as far away as it seems.

Grace Period

Ann met Wolfgang in Ohakune, and now they were in Queenstown, and there was nowhere left to go. A white van brought them to the bridge. Ann felt oddly calm during the drive, Wolfgang resting his hand on her thigh as they drove up through the bends to where the cliffs became canyon and the river below was green and narrow. The driver, a girl with bleached dreadlocks and a lip ring, said they were cute together and asked them how long they had been dating. "Oh, much time," Wolfgang said, winking, his tone facetious, as it always was, even when Ann wanted him to be serious. "Nine weeks," Ann said. She wondered if Wolfgang was surprised she knew, if anything could surprise him. It was nine weeks and three days, actually. Ann had been counting.

Ann's weight in kilos was written in Sharpie on her hand, and the girl was wrapping blue towels around her ankles. In an hour, Wolfgang would take a shuttle to the airport and fly to Christchurch, where a U.S. Air Force cargo plane would take him back to Antarctica for the summer. He was a scientist, researching the Ross Ice Shelf, which according to him, was melting and would go on melting until it was gone. "We study to predict, not change," he explained to Ann during one of their late-night talks in the courtyard of the hostel in Ohakune, Wolfgang spooning sweetened condensed milk from the can, the air crisp with the scent of carrot. "The future is decided," he said, grinning. "And it is wet!" Wolfgang was the only person Ann had met who was not afraid of the end of the world. Ann was afraid, though not of global warming so much as her college loans, which would go into effect when she returned home to Boston, and the job her father had set up for her at the medical device company he managed, answering phones with the other ladies in the back room. She had come to New Zealand because it was as far away as she could get.

The October day warmed as the sun lifted. Ann and Wolfgang sat on the wooden platform that perched over the drop, their legs straight out, while the girl and another worker fitted the straps around their shoulders and waists. Wolfgang tapped out a beat on Ann's thigh with his finger. Ann felt a twinge in the back of her throat, and the gush of saliva that preceded nausea. She fixed her eyes on a knot in the railing.

At the hostel in Ohakune, nine weeks back, Ann had lice, something she had picked up from City Stay in Auckland where the beds were pre-made with fitted sheets that had not smelled clean. She had been in New Zealand two weeks at that point and was already growing weary from the day-to-day routine of packing and unpacking, bus schedules, calling in reservations, sleeping with her passport and credit card and phone secured in the travel pouch against the skin of her belly. Beyond getting herself to the first hostel, Ann had not bothered to plan her trip. She wanted the adventure to happen to her. Instead, Ann found herself moving from town to town without purpose, feeling tired and out of place.

She met Wolfgang at breakfast. He was a large man, with blond curls that fell over his eyes, and looked to be somewhere in his thirties. He wore earbuds, his head bobbing as he ate a muffin. Ann sat a few seats down on the bench across from him.

"Do you like carrots?" he asked, pulling out one earbud so that it fell into his collar. Ann could hear the muted sound of heavy bass and drums.

"Yes?" she said.

"You know," he said, leaning closer as if telling a secret. "This place is the carrot capital of the world. Everything is carrot here. Muffin, bread, soup, beer. All carrot."

Ann looked at her muffin and saw the carrot shreds woven throughout and felt something move against her scalp. She had spent half the night trying to comb out the nits in the bathroom, washing them down the sink drain.

"I am Wolfgang, so you know," he said.

"Ann," she said.

"Ah, American!" he said. "Let me guess. Texas? Or is it New York City?"

"Boston, actually."

"Yes! Boston! Red Sox. Right?"

Ann nodded. "Where are you from?" He certainly wasn't a native, his accent sounding guttural, perhaps German.

Wolfgang bit into his muffin, chewed neatly, and swallowed. "Here and there."

"Have you been to Ohakune before?" Ann asked, sensing that was where he wanted the conversation to go.

Wolfgang looked up and tapped his finger on the table. A bearded man at the other end of the table crumpled his napkin and stood, leaving Ann and Wolfgang alone. "Six times," Wolfgang said, finally.

He went on to explain his job as a climate research scientist in Antarctica with NZARI. Each winter, he flew back to New Zealand and spent his time off traveling. He visited the same places every year. He started in the subtropical Northland, renting a surfboard in Coromandel, lounging in hot springs in Taupo, hiking in Ohakune, and slowly made his way to the South Island, and on to Queenstown, where he always did something "to make his blood pump"—one year white water rafting, one year skydiving, one year paragliding—and then took the express to Christchurch to depart for his post.

"You don't get tired of it?" Ann asked. She was irritated with her own homesickness which struck her, at times, out of nowhere, when seeing a blue sedan like her father drove, or smelling pine soap coming from a shower stall. She wondered if her father worried about her, since she had not called him. He had not called her, either. When her mother had become ill during Ann's freshman year in college, her father had stayed up nights researching alternative cures: acupuncture, macrobiotics, meditation, juicing. A year later, the prognosis terminal, he drove her to Houston because she was too sick to fly, to the Ayoub family home to see the weeping statues and paintings of Jesus, to touch the oily tears that had supposedly cured the Ayoub boy of stage four Leukemia. Ann couldn't believe it; her father hadn't been to church since he was a child. He'd expected a miracle. Afterwards, her mother gone, Ann's father retreated from her, though in ways only Ann could see. He continued to send checks and set up her dental visits every six months, but he did not worry if she missed her weekly call home. He did not get mad when she fell off the Dean's List and lost her partial scholarship. That piece of him had been used up. His new condo remained bare and smelled of the past tenant's dog. When Ann returned home, to her real life, she would live there, in the blank spare bedroom.

Wolfgang finished his muffin and wiped the crumbs into a pile. "No," he said. "This is my life. It's good for me."

Ann excused herself, thinking she should try to find a store within walking distance that carried lice treatment, and feeling that she had already said too much to this stranger whom she had spoken to more than anyone else she had met on her trip. Wolfgang winked. "Until next time," he said. Ann planned to leave Ohakune on a bus that afternoon.

The next morning, however, Ann woke in the same bed, in the same hostel. Wolfgang was eating another muffin when she entered the dining room, her hair wet on her shoulders from her shower. "I saved one for you," he said, pushing a muffin across the table. Ann sat. She hadn't expected to see Wolfgang again, but she had become lost yesterday while shopping, unsuccessfully, for lice shampoo, trying to use the snow dusted mountain in the background as her guide like the woman at the desk told her, and had missed her bus. She wondered if Wolfgang had seen her return. If she hadn't come to breakfast, would he have offered the muffin to someone else?

"You have time for hiking?" Wolfgang asked, though it didn't sound like a question. Ann tore a piece of her muffin, thinking of the bus ticket in her pocket and the next place she could go, and the place after that, and all of the places she would have to go before her trip ended and she had to return home.

"I do," she said.

They explored the forests at the base of Mt. Ruapehu that day, bringing slices of carrot bread from the hostel wrapped in napkins, and stopped to eat on a log near a creek, Wolfgang pointing out signs of disaster around them. "The trees grow so fast here, they fall over from their own weight," he said. "Just, zip and then—" His hand shot up and then slapped his thigh. "They are not native, not used to so much sun and water. Is not right." Ann imagined saplings giddy from abundance, spiraling toward the sun. "And the newts!" Wolfgang said. He whistled the sound of something falling to earth. "Don't even ask me about the newts."

"Doesn't it worry you?" Ann asked. She did not like to be reminded of all the ways in which the world was crumbling, even the mundane things, like how her father's hair had gone stark white since her mother's death, how Ann struggled not to sleep too much.

Wolfgang put his hand on her shoulder. "Everything is already decided," he said. He smiled, though Ann could see no trace of comedy in his eyes.

"With the climate, you mean?" she asked.

"Well, yes, that too. But not the point." He dipped a piece of carrot bread into a can of sweetened condensed milk that balanced on the log between them. "Free will? You know? It's a nice idea, but no."

"So, you're talking about predestination?" Ann thought of the elective class she had taken senior year on the Reformation, how she had only passed because the professor was a grandfatherly type who knew of her mother's death and pitied her. She'd spent most of that term asleep, often missing her alarm and her roommate's calls and not waking until lunch.

"Yes. Sure. Okay," Wolfgang said. "That's one word. I am scientist. I follow laws, same laws as universe follows, yes? Newtonian physics, Relativity, chemistry, all of these are rules, and we can predict outcome, and it is always the same. Are humans different? Not part of the universe? No. They are no different. Harder to predict, yes! Laws are not so easy to define. But all the same. We are not in charge. The laws are. So why worry?"

Ann scratched her head. She saw this belief thrilled Wolfgang.

Wolfgang finished the carrot bread, wiping the inside of the condensed milk can. He licked his fingers and raised the empty can above his head. "Okay, so, if I drop this can, what will happen?"

"It will fall."

"Right! It will fall at certain rate, nine point eight meters per second squared. Okay, give or take air resistance, right, which we could calculate too, no problem. So, if I have a calculator and meter stick, then right now I can predict how long it will take the can to hit the ground. Easy. Laws."

"But that's a tin can," Ann said. "Not a person."

"No? Okay, fine. So, what's in you? Let's see, oxygen, carbon, nitrogen, phosphorus, calcium." Wolfgang put down the can and pretended to write a list on his palm with his finger. "And these elements are made of atoms and atoms are made of subatomic particles and—"

Ann smiled, comforted by Wolfgang's confident enthusiasm. She wanted to rest her head in the shelter made by his hunching torso and close her eyes.

"Nothing special about humans," Wolfgang continued. "No separate rules. Laws tell us what will happen, and always right. So, science is not quite there yet with psychology, neurology, okay. But eventually. Someday we will have formulas to predict everything. What will I be when I grow up? Plug into formula! What car will I buy? Formula! The answers are there. Not to worry."

"You can make choices, though," Ann said. "I mean, I made the choice to come here, to go hiking with you." She stopped herself, realizing if things had gone as she had first expected, she would not be here with Wolfgang, and this realization made her feel special and lucky, as if meeting Wolfgang was the reason she was supposed to come to New Zealand in the first place.

"Maybe it feels like choice," he said. "But no. You were always going to be here. And now you are." He stood and extended his hand to help Ann up off the log. "Also," he said, "you have something in your hair."

That evening Wolfgang coated Ann's hair with mayonnaise in the bathroom at the hostel, and waited with her while the nits slowly suffocated, explaining to her the evolutionary necessity of parasites. The next day, he demonstrated how free will was an illusion by telling Ann she would go with him to Wellington, where they would catch the ferry to the South Island, in keeping with Wolfgang's usual schedule. "Do I have a choice?" Ann asked.

Wolfgang shook his head. "Is law of universe," he said.

THEIR ANKLE AND SIT STRAPS were tightened and now Ann and Wolfgang were standing backwards on the perch while the girl made her final checks. Below, in the river, a raft waited to retrieve them after the jump. Wolfgang was breathing heavily, and his T-shirt was damp at the neck. A gust of hot wind blew up from the canyon and Ann's nausea swelled with it, then passed. She wanted to unhook herself and leave, go back across the bridge and down into the cool forests where she would have more time to figure things out. Wolfgang's face shone with excitement for what was about to come.

On the ferry to the South Island, Wolfgang and Ann stood on the upper deck and watched dolphins jump in the surf. They took a train to Christchurch and stayed in Wolfgang's reserved single room at the hostel, a massive brick building that ran along a city block. After they had slept together for the first time, Wolfgang opened a can of sweetened condensed milk from the stash he kept in his backpack and shared it with Ann. "Every year I do this, and every year the same. But this year, you!" It felt generous, coming from Wolfgang, though the implication became clearer as their travels continued. Wolfgang never veered from his itinerary, despite Ann asking once if they could detour to a bed and breakfast that advertised the most luxurious beds. "I'm sorry," he said. "That is not the way I go."

In Oamaru they saw little blue penguins waddle across the beach in the rain. It had been four weeks since they met, and they were making their way down the east coast of the South Island following Wolfgang's usual plan. They sat on wooden bleachers with the other onlookers, the wet nylon of their windbreakers swishing as their arms touched. Wolfgang laughed each time a penguin shot out of its pen and across the sand to the water and Ann felt his ribs buckle. She wished she could be as lighthearted, but she was already thinking about the end, when Wolfgang would have to return to Antarctica and she would have to go back to Boston. Wolfgang gave no indication that his plans would change. Whatever would happen had already been decided, at least according to Wolfgang. Ann could only wait and see.

That night they stayed in a small room with wood paneling and a rocking chair and a space heater. They showered and started their laundry in the coin-op in the basement, and got into the twin bed, where Wolfgang read and Ann lay with her head on his chest. She imagined the two of them getting an apartment in the country where they could go hiking and grow herbs in window boxes and adopt a cat, and Wolfgang could study the rising ocean levels and, on the weekends, campaign against invasive newts. She would keep cans of sweetened condensed milk in the pantry for him. Her school loans might not find her there. Maybe her father could visit.

"I can feel your heartbeat," Ann said, her hand on Wolfgang's bare sternum with its cluster of light hair.

"I should hope so," he said.

"I mean," she said. "I feel close to you." It was so hard for her to talk to Wolfgang in any serious way.

"No room in this bed. So we must be close."

"Don't go back," Ann said. She pushed up from Wolfgang's chest and accidentally jabbed him in the ribs with her elbow, and he winced.

"To work?"

"Yes. To Antarctica. Don't go. Stay here with me."

"But it's my job," he said. He rubbed his rib.

"So?" Ann said. "Can't you get another job?"

"Why another job? I like my job."

"But what about me?"

"I like you!"

"Won't you miss me?"

"Yes, of course! I will miss you."

"Then why can't you stay?"

Wolfgang paused, raising his eyebrows. "Because my job?"

Ann pushed the covers off and stood up. She pulled on her jeans and jacket and took her travel pouch with her passport and credit card. "Forget it. I'm going for a walk."

Outside, the rain had turned to mist. Ann walked straight in one direction, afraid of getting lost, crossing cobblestone roads and passing bars alive with music and voices. How could she ask Wolfgang to make a choice for her when he didn't even believe in choice? Or was that what he told all the women he met? And how many women had come before? Wolfgang gave no details of his past winters, aside from what activities he did and where to get the best fish and chips, though back in Invercargill, where Wolfgang and Ann had stood on a windy beach and looked out toward Stewart Island and beyond to where Antarctica lay, Ann had sworn she saw the hostel receptionist smile too warmly at Wolfgang when she welcomed him back. For all Ann knew, Wolfgang had a girlfriend in Antarctica, too. Ann had no one else. She had nothing beyond this time with Wolfgang. Her father had called this trip her grace period, and in a literal sense it was true because her loan repayment had not yet begun. But she knew what her father meant, that her travels were a short hiatus from the laws of adulthood. She was allowed to visit but not to stay.

Ann walked quickly, warmth spreading through her limbs. The night sky lifted above her. After walking long enough to cross many small streets, Ann approached an intersection where two main roads crossed at a traffic light, and beyond it the buildings grew larger and further apart. She hesitated to go on, but she was not ready to go back. If Wolfgang was correct, her fate had already been decided, set into motion at the beginning of the universe. An atom of carbon decayed or didn't decay, and millions of years later Ann fell off her bike at age seven, breaking her wrist. Sodium bonded to magnesium and a boy in Texas was cured of leukemia. A star exhausted its hydrogen, and Ann's mother died. The laws were responsible. Only the laws.

Ann listened to the peel of tires on the damp pavement, feeling with her toes the edge of the curb. She closed her eyes. When the street became quiet, she stepped out into it. If she was meant to be here with Wolfgang, the universe would show her.

The sound of cars started up again, their motion parallel to her, and Ann tensed, but did not open her eyes. A car honked and Ann felt a spray of moisture on her legs and the whoosh of air quite close to her body. Then another car, close enough for Ann to hear the song from its radio. She walked faster, one hand out in front as if to shield herself. Ann wanted to believe as Wolfgang did; she wanted to have faith, but she was scared. Hadn't her mother believed the universe would save her from the cancer? And yet it had sided with the disease. Another car passed in front of her, the driver yelling "What are you doing?" and Ann opened her eyes in time to avoid tripping on the curb and stepped up onto the sidewalk. Horns continued to chastise her as the line of cars finished. She let them. What she had done was senseless and yet she was perfectly fine. The universe had made its point.

When she got back to the hostel, Ann's hair was wet against her face. Wolfgang was listening to his music and folding a pile of their laundry onto the rocking chair, carefully matching her socks and rolling them into balls. "You look like a blue penguin," he said, pointing to her lips which had gone purple. He opened his arms and Ann walked into them, her anger replaced by a flat kind of happiness.

It would have happened that night, Ann later calculated. Wolfgang had always been careful before, stringently so, but Ann told him it was okay and he believed her, though what she meant was something else. What she meant was everything was okay, because it would have to be, since she was unable to change it. Afterwards, Ann did not feel the worry she expected to, but instead a relief that something had been done that could not be undone. A choice had been made, if only by fate.

"WHAT YOU'RE GOING TO DO IS COUNT TO THREE," the girl told them. Ann and Wolfgang were side by side, hooked together by a clip at their waist. "Then you're going to tip back, or jump, whichever, but you should agree on it."

Wolfgang looked at Ann. "Do you want to jump?" he asked.

"Okay," Ann said, her voice barely working. She wasn't sure she could do it. Everything was quiet, except the breeze that whistled through the posts of the bridge.

"Is easier backwards," Wolfgang said.

Ann nodded. Her throat was tight.

"You want to do it, still? Yes?"

Ann looked down.

"You don't have to."

When would she tell him? After the jump he would be celebratory and there would be so much to do, the packing and phone calls and getting to the shuttle on time. It wasn't as if she believed it would change his mind. To be certain, she had bought a test at the Pak-n-Save last night, while Wolfgang used the Wi-Fi in the common area to finalize his flight. Her roommate in college had needed a test once, too, and Ann remembered sitting on the tiled floor of the dorm bathroom with her while the two minutes passed, waiting for the sign.

"Ready?" asked the girl.

Wolfgang grinned.

"No," Ann said.

"What?" Wolfgang asked.

"I'm not ready," she said. "Wait."

Another couple was walking across the bridge, beginning their preparations. How could Ann say anything with the girl staring at them, checking her watch. There was no time. It was already over. It was over before they came to the bridge, and before Ann got the test, and before they slept, last night, cramped together in one bunk in the bunk room because the hostel didn't have private rooms and Wolfgang needed to be close to the bus stop. During the night Ann had woken up to see a man stagger to the doorway and urinate on the floor, leaving a sodden circle in the carpet that Ann was careful to step over in the morning. This was not the way it was supposed to end.

Wolfgang put his hand on Ann's cheek. "Is going to be okay, you know? One blink and done."

"I know," Ann said.

"I do many times. Very safe."

"Okay."

The girl clapped. "Count to three!"

"One!" Wolfgang said. He grasped Ann's hand. She felt faint and detached from her body. After her mother died, Ann had dreams of jumping off ledges into blackness, as if trying to join her mother in death, and now felt like one of those dreams.

"Two!" Wolfgang said.

Ann leaned back and dropped from the ledge before Wolfgang could finish. He let out a scream that Ann barely heard. The rushing air in her ears was louder than she had expected. Wolfgang was plummeting with her, pulled down by her motion, and he let go of her hand to claw at the air. Ann was smiling. She had surprised him. It was all gravity and air resistance now. The laws of the universe working themselves out.

Lucky

Rhea was forty when she became lucky. That was the year Logan arrived, bringing his *Thomas the Tank Engine* book with its chewed cardboard pages and a plastic grocery bag of clothes. Her brother dropped the boy on her doorstep like a package. Rhea hated how much she could see her brother in Logan's small face, the dark eyes and sharp chin that made her brother appear snake-ish and cruel. The boy bit his book and watched her.

Her brother did not come back that first week when Rhea spent each night in the recliner with Logan clutched to her neck and all the lights on in the house, a Newport turning to ash between her fingers. He did not come back five months later, when Rhea signed the guardianship papers, or a year after that, the day Logan cracked his head on the corner of a wall, and she learned he was blind in one eye and required corrective lenses. Because Logan could not remember the man but only that he had existed, Rhea told him his father was a policeman who had died protecting a family from robbers. She chose policeman because it was the opposite of her brother, who had been arrested more times than Rhea could count and would likely end up incarcerated, if he wasn't already. Upon hearing the news, Logan stared at the wall and held his breath, as he did when trying to understand something new. A moment later, he exhaled and went to

Rhea, pressing his forehead into her upper arm. "Don't be sad, now," Rhea said. "You're lucky. You have me. Plenty of kids don't have fathers."

But Rhea was the one with luck. She discovered it, the summer after Logan moved in, wedged into the space between her belly button and rib cage while pushing a cart at the Food King. Logan, who was almost four and too large for the baby seat where he sat, the tips of his light-up sneakers smacking Rhea's thighs, was sucking on his sleeve and humming the *Thomas* song when Rhea felt the first spasm, as if her insides were being tugged. She planted her feet and thrust out her jaw, defiantly confronting the pain in the same way she confronted the stares Logan elicited from other shoppers. In front of shelves of Jell-O, Rhea squatted as the tugging wrenched, and there on the floor at her feet was a gold charm bracelet. Immediately, Rhea felt a wave of relief and the cooling flush of sweat. The chain was heavier than she expected, the tiny heart and key charms dotted in diamonds. Logan pulled his sleeve from his mouth and reached for the bracelet and Rhea let him rub it against his wet chin. She looked around to see if anyone had seen.

The man at the pawn shop gave Rhea a thousand dollars for the bracelet, which she used to buy herself a six-month supply of Newports before the tax went up again and a Big Wheels trike and a beagle puppy for Logan, whom he named Shrek. Four months later, the luck returned. Rhea was pumping gas, and to relieve the spasm she picked up a soggy scratch ticket that had been dropped to the concrete island. It was a winner, unclaimed. Two weeks later, Tom Ford sunglasses in the parking lot in front of CVS. On those days, Rhea and Logan would get take-out from Deng's and eat on the living room floor watching the Game Show channel, Shrek licking Logan's greasy fingers.

Mostly, they were able to get by on what Rhea made working at the nursing home. They lived in the house Rhea's parents left her—both of them gone to cancer within a year of each other—a brown split-level with wall-to-wall carpeting that held the scent of her mother's beef stew and her father's Pall Malls. Her brother inherited her father's cherry red Chevelle, which he ran into a tree a week after the funeral. Every few months, when Rhea cycled into worry that her brother would suddenly show up, once again, on her doorstep, this time to take the boy from her, she made a phone call to the only place he ever worked, Bernie's Grill, and pretended to be a debt collector in need of his forwarding address. Last she heard, her brother was living in a halfway house in Bangor, Maine, which sounded very far away, to Rhea. She put two stamps on the letter she wrote to him there, to make certain he would receive the message that stated he had no rights to Logan, at least not as far as she was concerned. She almost included a school picture of the boy, eyes pinched in a grin behind thick glass, as evidence that Rhea was doing just fine raising him, but she couldn't bring herself to part with the image. Her brother did not deserve to see it.

 The year Logan was nine and repeating the fourth grade, Rhea found a wallet under a chair at the DMV, where she was waiting with Logan to register the pickup she had bought at auction. Rhea put the wallet into the pouch of her sweatshirt and pressed it against her belly. With her other hand, she pulled Logan into the restroom, where she told him to wash his hands while she examined the wallet, not meeting Logan's gaze reflected in the mirror. Wetting her thumb on her tongue, Rhea fanned through the twenties. She slipped the cash under the waistband of her jeans and pulled her sweatshirt down over it, then ripped several paper towels from the dispenser for Logan to dry his hands.

 "Now, take this to the lady at the desk," she said, handing the wallet to Logan.

 "Why?" he asked.

"Go on." She turned him around and gave him a small push through the restroom door. After a moment, she followed.

"Did you take any money out of this?" the woman at the desk was asking. She opened the wallet. Logan was holding his breath.

"It's okay if you did, honey. Just hand it over to me now and I won't say anything."

Rhea swallowed a cough. She came up behind Logan and held his shoulders, gripping tightly to stop her shaking hands. "Is there a problem?"

The woman sat up straighter. "Ma'am, this wallet was reported missing earlier today. Five hundred dollars in it, and he's telling me there was nothing?"

"Are you calling him a liar?"

The woman blinked. "Are you lying, son?"

Logan's face was blotching red, his blind eye crossing just slightly into the corner of its socket. The guidance counselor from Logan's school had recommended a neuropsychological evaluation, but Rhea did not need some overpaid doctor telling her what she already knew, that Logan was a slow learner, and you might have to tell him the same thing several times before it sunk in, which was part of him in the same way that lying was part of her brother—a congenital defect, and nothing to be helped.

Rhea coughed into her shoulder. "Can't you see you're scaring him," she said. The bills pressed into her belly, dampening from sweat. She had not been challenged in her luck before. It made her want the money even more, as if her misfortune to suffer this indignity directly correlated to her entitlement of the reward. It was not altogether different from the way she felt about Logan each time she reminded herself her brother could come and take him back.

"I'm going to have to call security," the woman said. She picked up her telephone receiver and held it in the crook of her neck while she dialed.

Logan exhaled all at once. He squirmed in Rhea's hold. "But," he said. Rhea squeezed his shoulders with her fingernails, unsure what the boy might admit. She was spinning, dizzy from how quickly the situation had gotten away from her. Before Logan could say another word, Rhea pulled him backwards and toward the exit. The woman hung up and watched them leave, as if daring Rhea to lift her sweatshirt and reveal the money. Rhea paused in the doorway while Logan went to the truck, then pointed her finger.

"Bitch," she said, as loudly as she could.

That night, while they ate lo mein and crab rangoons at the living room coffee table, Logan began to cry. "Are we going to jail?" he asked.

Rhea's lungs seized and she forced down a cough. "Come again?"

"Because you stole the money," Logan said.

"I am not a thief." Rhea pushed her plate to the center of the table where the dog couldn't get at it and patted her pockets to find her cigarettes. Her hands shook.

"But you take things that don't belong to you," he said. Rhea leaned back against the couch and bit on a cigarette, lighting it using both hands on the lighter. Inside she was spinning again, as she had been at the DMV.

"I am not a thief," she repeated. She took quick drags of the cigarette until her ears buzzed. "Did I steal that wallet today?"

Logan's eyes stopped watering. "No," he said. "But."

"And did I steal the credit cards inside? Or the social security card? Did I do that, Logan? Did I?"

"No."

Rhea dragged hard on the cigarette, her cheeks hollowing. She flicked ash into an empty take-out carton. "Okay, now. And you returned the wallet, safe and sound, to that very unpleasant lady at the desk. So what if a little cash fell out? Should I go to jail for being a helpful citizen?"

Logan stared at the wall.

"Should I?"

The boy was holding his breath. She snapped her fingers in front of his face. "Well?"

"Okay," he said, a rush of air.

"Okay what? I should go to jail?"

"I mean, no. No."

"Are you sure about that?"

Logan rubbed his nose. "No. I mean yes." He inhaled with a shudder, and his face screwed up again, the tears coming silently, now. "I don't know."

Rhea's anger drained. Ash fell onto her fingers as the cigarette burned to the filter. She clenched her teeth. She was all the boy had, and he knew it. "Well, that's fine," she said, pulling another cigarette from the pack with unsteady fingers. "You know right from wrong. Of course you do." She could not bear to have Logan think of her as a criminal. Her brother was a criminal. Rhea was lucky.

Logan pressed his eyes with the heels of his hands. "Sorry, Rhea," he said.

"Don't be stupid," Rhea said. She cleared her throat, hearing the teary thickness of it. "Nothing to be sorry for. A little policeman, you are," she added, and just like that, Logan's face lifted and his eyes shone.

YEARS PASSED. Rhea and Logan lived in a pattern of scarcity punctuated by sudden wealth, Rhea's luck arriving with enough frequency to keep them afloat. There was a set of hearing aids on a chair in the pharmacy waiting section, a lapis lazuli tie clip in an elevator, a solid gold toe ring at the beach. Rhea's brother never came, though anytime a red car pulled into the driveway to turn around, or a delivery man knocked at the front door when Rhea wasn't expecting it, she turned to ice.

On the morning of his high school graduation, Rhea woke up to find Logan already showered and working to button the cuffs of his white dress shirt while Shrek chewed his paws at the boy's feet. Logan had grown round in face and body, and his glasses had grown even thicker to keep his bad eye from drifting away on its own. Rhea stood behind him with an unlit cigarette in her lips, her heart swelling into her throat. She reached for his buttons.

Once Logan was ready, Rhea turned to herself. In the back of her closet she found an outfit of her mother's that she kept only because she couldn't stand to throw it away, a high-waisted dress made of corduroy that her mother would wear when she had to go anywhere of any significance, such as a sit-down restaurant or to court to watch Rhea's brother lie in front of the judge. The dress was tight, but it fit. It fell close enough to her ankles so her sneakers could barely be seen.

The ceremony was in the auditorium of the new high school, which had been built well after Rhea had completed her four years at the now abandoned building across town. Rhea had been there only a handful of times for Logan's yearly IEP meetings, during which Logan's teachers and guidance counselors tried to convince her that Logan's inability to test proficiently was something she should worry about, as if they knew him better. She took a seat near the back, alone in her row. The other parents and relatives stood and sat in groups, chatting and laughing with each other and looking through Rhea as if she were invisible. She wanted a cigarette.

The crowd quieted as the band began to play "Pomp and Circumstance," and the lights dimmed and spotlights shone on the graduates who were marching in, two by two, their white, polyester gowns swishing as they made their way to the stage. Rhea squinted to see where Logan fell in line but could not find him. The teenagers carried squares of poster board, and when they took their positions on the risers, they flipped their signs to reveal painted black lettering. Rhea wondered, at first, if they were protesting, but as she focused on the words, she saw one read "Pediatrician," held by a petite girl with tightly curled hair. Another read "World Traveler." A boy with a nose ring had "Organic Farmer." Rhea did recall a note sent home explaining that the students would be thinking about, and then sharing, the person they hoped to become after graduation, though she had forgotten to ask Logan about it. She had not understood the purpose. It struck her as preposterous. Why did Logan need to become someone new after graduation? Rhea would be happy if he stayed exactly who he was.

Then she saw him, as he finally passed by, the last one in line and unpaired, as alone as Rhea was. Logan grinned proudly at Rhea and she gave him a thumbs up, though she was looking at his backwards piece of poster board and wondering what was on the other side. He positioned himself on the bottom riser and flipped his sign and held it up to his chin. Rhea wished for it to be blank. But it wasn't blank. The sign said "Polissman."

The audience grew silent. Rhea coughed. Her neck pulsed and her dress became an oven. A burst of female laughter fluttered and then abruptly hushed. Why hadn't anyone helped him spell the word correctly? Would that have been so hard? Principal Garney took the podium and parents murmured and clapped and several more giggled. Rhea worked her jaw. She was shaking. No one was looking and yet she could sense them judging her, somehow, and blaming her for raising a child to believe something ridiculous, that he was capable of becoming a policeman when he couldn't even spell the word.

A cough clawed its way out, and then another, and Rhea pressed her lips together. Up on the risers, Logan was pushing the top of his sign into his neck as if he were trying to cut off his head. Principal Garney was talking about solid foundations and bright futures, and parents were filming with their phones. Rhea had to leave. She hoped Logan wouldn't see her as she went out the side exit into the front entryway of the school, one hand over her mouth. Outside, in the parking lot, she allowed the coughing fit to come, bracing herself with her palms on her thighs. When she righted, her vision was blurry but further off in the parking lot, leaning on the hood of a cherry red car, Rhea saw a man and the man was watching her. He had dark hair, like Logan, which was pulled behind his ears.

It's him, she thought. After all this time, he's come.

Rhea lit a cigarette, coughing on the first inhale. The smoke grounded her, though her lungs itched as if to burst. She squinted at the man, who had not moved. *Polissman*. It was just like her brother to show up after years of silence, expecting nothing to have changed because he had not changed, because he was not capable of change. Rhea coughed again, then spit. She bit her cigarette and pulled up the hem of her skirt and began walking into the parking lot, toward the man. The man watched her come. *Polissman*, she thought again, and she felt angry, and the anger was for everyone who had ever failed Logan and the person who had failed him the most was her brother, and now Rhea was quite certain she would fight him, if that's what it took. She would not let him near the boy.

"You can't see him, Richie," Rhea said through her teeth as she moved closer to the man. She dropped her hem and took the cigarette from her mouth and coughed into her fist. "I won't allow it."

The man held a phone. Rhea could see, now, that he had not been staring at her but at his phone which was pointed in her general direction. Was he filming her? When Richie was fourteen and she was twenty-six he had used her identity to apply for multiple credit cards and ran up a balance that destroyed her credit for years. Maybe he had a new plan that involved posting a video of her online and then getting her to pay him to take it down; it wouldn't surprise her.

"Logan thinks you're dead, if you must know. I told him you were a hero." Rhea finished her cigarette and flicked the butt toward the man. "So, you're welcome."

The man looked up from his phone, smiling blandly. He pulled one bud from his ear. "Excuse me?"

"Don't play that game with me," Rhea said. How many times had Richie looked right at her, without seeing her? The first time her parents put him in the hospital it was Rhea who went to visit him in that sweaty little room with metal chairs in front of a chained-up television, and he wouldn't even speak to her. Not one word, as if she hadn't driven two hours to get there, as if she hadn't smuggled in a package of Nutter Butters because they were once his favorite. "You have no right to be here, no right at all. What have you done for the boy in all these years? What's one thing?"

The man shook his head. "Can I help you?"

Rhea cocked her head and tapped her forehead. "Come again? Can you help me? No, I don't think you can. It's too late for that. I fed him, Richie. I clothed him. I gave him a roof over his head, a bed. A dog!"

The man pulled the other bud from his ear and stood up from the hood of the car, which Rhea could now see was not so much cherry red as stop sign red, and a Nissan. "Hey, lady, I'm just waiting for my cousin."

"He's graduating today, Richie. Do you know what that means?"

The man thumbed something into his phone.

"Look at me!"

The man looked. Rhea searched for a sign of recognition in his eyes. She wanted to reach out, shake him, hug him, slap him into familiarity. She wanted him to tell her she had done a good job with the boy, because suddenly she wasn't sure if she had, she wasn't sure at all. She knew only one thing, that she had loved the boy more than anything else. That much, she had done. It was such a small thing.

"It means I did okay, Richie. I did my best. I made mistakes, I know that." Rhea looked down at her dress and saw the scuffed toes of her sneakers and thought *polissman*. Logan's guidance counselor had suggested adult residency services for when Logan turned twenty-two; it was a few years off, but the wait list was long, at least for the better places. Just the phrase *better places* made Rhea's hands turn to fists. "You can screw yourself," she had said to the counselor, whom she never liked.

Yes, there had been mistakes.

The man blew air through his mouth. "Okay, sure." He reached for the car door handle.

"No, Richie, it's not okay. It's not okay at all." Rhea suddenly remembered that the boy was inside the auditorium, up on that stage, still holding that terrible sign, probably. Had the principal called his name yet? She needed to go back. What would he do if he looked out into that snickering crowd and did not see one familiar face? Who would clap for him? And, in that moment, Rhea saw Logan's face as he flipped his sign, the proud set of eyes behind those glasses, his love for a father who'd never existed. Rhea had lied to the boy, and that could not be undone. She felt the familiar pain in her gut that usually indicated imminent luck, and yet she had a sense not of good fortune but of the opposite, of having stolen something that she could not give back.

The man was in his car and reversing out of his parking spot. As he drove away he put his arm out the window and thrust his middle finger at her. Rhea gathered herself to scream but what came out, instead, was a small cough. The man sped through the lot, turned onto the street and was gone.

Rhea lit another cigarette and stood there, watching the place where the car had once been. She rubbed the spot in her stomach that throbbed with promise, though there was nothing to be found on the pavement around her.

The man wasn't her brother. She knew that.

Her stomach cramped, and she thought, again, of Logan. Richie was not coming back, not today and not ever. She also knew this.

Someday she would tell the boy the truth, that Richie did not deserve him, and perhaps Rhea did not, either. But now her stomach was pulling her back, toward the boy. Toward her luck. What she would find there, she didn't know. But it would belong to her.

The Principle

Six weeks into our new life, Minnow peels a strip of sunburned skin from his shoulder and asks me if I need to pull over for lunch. He's driving his dead parents' Bentley, and I feel its tight roar as the transmission downshifts and we speed past an RV in the right lane. I am hungry, but Minnow is just hitting his stride, soaring actually, so I shake my head and light a clove cigarette. Minnow grins, his broken front tooth flashing, dimples carving commas in his cheeks. I hope he took his meds today. I usually make him open his mouth and lift his tongue, but this morning, after waking up at a rest stop, I'd only watched him chase the pills with a sip of four-day old coffee from the Bentley's cupholder and then put the orange bottles back into my bag. I feel drained and damp, itchy from the chigger bites covering my midsection, and when I roll down my window, hot air blasts through the car and dulls the sweaty sheen on my skin. The Bentley is still accelerating.

It is August and we are driving east on I-80, headed for Washington County Maine for the blueberry harvest, which, Minnow assures me, will be better than detasseling corn in Nebraska, cooler and less muddy. Minnow and I have been together five months, since we met at the Goodwill in Adams, when I was living with my mother again. I was trying to stay busy while my mother was at work, and I was looking through the furniture section for a lamp to brighten her new condo. Minnow was pulling vintage Levis from a rack. Even though it had been a few years, I recognized his face from the Xtreme Winter commercials that used to run on the local stations back when I was in high school, the ones that showed Minnow polishing snowboards in the background while his father advertised the "finest winter sports equipment in the Berkshires." Minnow's family was famous in Adams. Everyone knew that his parents' Cessna went down over Denali last year. I'd felt awful for him, then, reading the article about how it had taken rescue crews two weeks to reach the bodies due to weather. Minnow must have sensed me staring at him, there in the Goodwill; he must have known that I wasn't the only person at the store wondering why he was buying secondhand pants. When he met my eyes, his face looked nothing like that smiling teenage boy in the commercials. It was open and troubled like my father's had been, but questioning too, as if he needed something from me. Maybe he could tell I knew what it meant to lose a parent. Later, after I moved into Minnow's giant house with him, I would look back on our meeting as if it were destiny. I said this one day, after we had attempted to make love, and he had rolled to the side of the bed, staring at his phone. He'd pretended not to hear me, but that didn't make it any less true.

Six weeks ago, Minnow came home from his monthly appointment with Dr. Franz, tossed a new prescription next to where I was lying on his bed and said, "Shell, this life is for shitheads. We're leaving." He was tired of being Dr. Franz's psychopharmaceutical guinea pig, which got worse after his parents died and the old meds stopped cutting it, and I was tired of having to explain myself to my mother, watching the lines between my eyes grow more permanent, just like hers. So this is how we are living now: sleeping in tents and hotels, working on farms, pulling the tassels off the tops of corn stalks so they can't fertilize each other. We locked up Minnow's house and left a key for the accountant who was supposed to come by once a week to make sure the cat wasn't dead. Minnow said we would start fresh. We would follow the Hindu principle of Ahimsa: non-harm. The night before we left, I called my mother, and she was silent for so long I thought the call had dropped and then she told me she didn't know how much longer she could watch me do this kind of thing.

"What kind of thing?" I said, but the call really had dropped, or she'd hung up. When I called back, she let the phone go to voicemail, which I never leave.

BY THREE IN THE AFTERNOON, the gas light is on. We are somewhere in Iowa. Around us, soybean fields stretch endlessly, the stubby plants gleaming like the surface of water. Minnow pulls into an Exxon. He stands shirtless and barefoot in one of my peasant skirts he took to wearing in the cornfields because jeans were too hot, while gas gulps through the hose into the Bentley's large tank. After a month of driving cornfields, the car still looks regal, but the hubcaps and one side mirror are gone, and mud splatter covers the grill and the winged "B" emblem on the front. Sometimes the engine dies and won't restart without a jump. That happened last night in Elkhorn after we left the detasseling camp, and if we hadn't been within walking distance of a gas station we might have been in trouble because another thing about this new life is Minnow doesn't want us to have cell phones. He threw his under a combine and tossed our chargers out the window of the Bentley. I still have my iPhone, but only about a third of the battery is left.

I go around the side of the gas station and find a bathroom. Inside, I pee and wash my hands for a long time in warm water, trying to scrub off the sticky gray rings around my fingers left over from the duct tape I wore when detasseling.

The tassels burn like rope if you don't get a good grip on them. My hands should have toughened up by now, according to Minnow, but they are blistered and raw. Minnow has toughened up. Three days ago, in Nebraska, he spread-eagled out of the back of the crew leader's pickup while we were driving to a field and fell on a rock and broke his front tooth. He spit on the ground and laughed, as if it was nothing. He wasn't this way before, so frenetic all the time, reckless. But, in our new life, Minnow doesn't take all of Dr. Franz's drugs, except for the ones I make him take. When my father went off his mood stabilizers, that's when things got worse, but Minnow hates them because of the side effects, mainly impotence. We've only had sex four times, and three of those times were when we first got to Nebraska, before I realized that Minnow was going pure. Now I put the pills into a plastic cough syrup cup each morning and I watch Minnow take them. Nurse Shell, he says.

Outside the bathroom, I see Minnow at the pump, washing the Bentley's windshield and squeegee-ing intently. I reach for my phone and bring up my mother's number. I put my finger over the green call button. I've rehearsed what I will say: first, that I'm sorry for leaving, again, even though I promised I wouldn't do this anymore. Then I will tell my mother I have a new life now, and Minnow and I are taking care of each other, without asking for anything from anyone. I'll say this time it's going to be okay.

After that, she'll say, that Minnow, such a strange name. It's awful about his parents but he's no good for you. Don't you think I can tell? Don't you think I learned something from your father's death? And then we'll both pause over the word *death*, letting it take up the space between us, as though what my father did to himself can be described that way. I imagine that, here, my mother will sniff, and I will know that she is pinching her earlobe the way we both do when we're worried, and when she says that she really shouldn't have bailed me out after what happened last year with Ryan in Montreal, I'll press the red button and I won't feel guilty.

When I turn back to Minnow, I see him flapping his arms and talking to a man in a John Deere cap. The man doesn't look happy. I put my phone back into my pocket, grateful I haven't wasted much of the charge.

"Shell," Minnow says, putting his arm around me and dimpling with tense charm. "This gentleman right here just asked how a kid like me could end up with a car like this. Would you care to explain it to him?"

I look at the man, who has backed up to the door of his F-150. "Can't take a joke, I guess," he says. He looks nervous and I wonder what else Minnow has said to him.

"Stop it," I say. "No harm, remember?"

Minnow cracks a wide grin at the man. He swishes his skirt and wiggles his fingers. "Shithead."

The man slams his door and drives off.

"What does he know about me?" Minnow says. He starts to get into the car, then stands up again and slaps the roof of the Bentley. "What does he know about us, Shell?"

I shake my head. Neither of us looks like we should be driving a Bentley, or an F-150 for that matter. Nobody out here knows about the Xtreme Winter franchise, or that Minnow got his nickname from a fly-fishing trip in the Rockies he'd gone on with his dad and the CEO of some yogurt company when Minnow was eight. No one knows he used to be on TV, the richest kid around, his smile unbroken.

"Let me drive for a while?" I tease. I know he won't let me, he says no one can drive the Bentley but him, but I want to distract him. I grab the keys in his fist.

It works. Minnow laughs and pretends to karate kick me. I jab him in the chest. We scuffle for a minute until Minnow grabs me and hugs me so tight I can feel his heart beating through his bare chest. I fall back against the side of the car, holding him, his weight pulling on me. His breath is in my ear. I rub his back, his spine knobby like a child's. When he releases, he looks at me so seriously it's as though he's about to tell me the biggest secret of his life. But then the seriousness lifts, and Minnow exhales.

"Give me the keys," he says.

FIVE HOURS LATER, I am in the back seat digging through the pile of clothes for one of Minnow's cleaner shirts. "Restaurant or gas station?" he asks over his shoulder. He has agreed to break for dinner, since we've already cleared six hundred miles today and we just passed Chicago. I am so hungry that each cigarette I smoke makes me dizzy. I think if I stood up, I'd faint. I pick out a blue button-down shirt with armpit stains.

"Restaurant," I say. "I want air conditioning. And real food." I climb back to the front and hold the shirt in my lap.

"Sorry," he says, sincerely. "I didn't notice how late it was. You're probably ready for a big juicy hamburger by now." I laugh because Minnow has decided that eating meat is another thing we aren't doing in our new life; it is part of the principle we are following. Minnow read about it in a biography about George Harrison. No meat, no alcohol, no drugs, no violence. We gave up drinking and switched from the Camels we used to smoke to Djarum clove cigarettes, which seem less toxic and have sweet, honey-dipped filters. Minnow used to get in fights a lot, especially after his parents died, though as long as I've been with him he's been okay, even if I have been worried about him lately. The principle means something to him. I think it reminds him that we are starting over, and that this time we will do things the right way.

Minnow puts his right hand on my neck and pulls me toward him. I can smell the chlorine in his hair, left over from the town pool in Elkhorn where we'd swim most nights after detasseling, even if it meant jumping the fence to get in.

"Maybe some ribs, too," I add.

"Wings."

"Hmm. Fried chicken."

"Meatloaf." Minnow's hand moves down my back and hooks around my waist.

"Steak tips," I say. He pulls me up against the center console. My thigh hurts where it's pressing into the cup holders, but I try not to show it. "No, veal."

"Sure, and maybe some duckling or kitten or something, you know, on the side." Minnow laughs and tries to lift me over the console. My seatbelt stretches and my knee hits the gearshift. I push myself up, and Minnow pulls my left leg onto his lap, running his hand up the inside of my thigh. I hunch down, worried we might get pulled over. I think about the meds, again, trying to remember if I saw Minnow swallow this morning, or if he got out of the car and went into the restroom right after.

"Come here," he says, and kisses me, hard and wet, on my cheek, his eyes squeezed shut. The car starts to drift into the passing lane and behind us a car lays on its horn. I grab the wheel. Minnow's eyes are still closed and he's pressing on the gas.

"You'll make us crash!" I scream. I am holding the wheel with both hands. Slowly, Minnow opens his eyes, still focused on me. He winks. He squeezes the inside of my thigh so hard I know it will bruise. He reaches for the wheel. I jump into my seat, the seat belt snapping back. Minnow is laughing.

"That wasn't funny. We could have died."

"Nah," Minnow says. "It was funny. I knew you'd save us."

THE ONLY RESTAURANT IN CURTAINS, ILLINOIS, is the Jackalope Lodge. It's a rustic building with a neon sign that reads "a place for the whole family" above a bust of a horned rabbit. Inside, there are deer heads on the wall, a foosball table and an ancient Duck Hunt video game, and two men sitting at the bar. Minnow and I choose a booth. His shirt is buttoned in two places, hanging open at his chest. We are both wearing peasant skirts knotted at the hems to make them easier to detassel in. Neither of us has had a proper shower in weeks. After a few minutes, the waitress from behind the bar comes out with menus. Her rabbit-shaped nametag says Cassie.

Cassie sets down our menus. She takes a folded piece of paper from her back pocket and scribbles on it with her pen. I notice that her eyes are so green they look fake, like apple Jolly Ranchers, and I almost want to ask her if they're real or contacts, but I'm staring at her too long so I look away.

"Drinks?" she asks.

I start to shake my head, but then Minnow says "Why not?" We search for our IDs. "We've earned it," he continues. "We've been driving all day."

"Okay," I say, though it makes me nervous. He shouldn't drink with his meds.

Cassie sees our out-of-state IDs and exhales loudly. They are Massachusetts issued; Minnow's shows a picture of him before he grew out his hair. Macalister Jenkins, it says, aged twenty-four. Same age as me. Cassie flips over the cards and then holds them up to the light, squinting. "Kenny?" she yells, and a man in an apron comes out from a door behind the bar.

"What the fuck. They're not fake," Minnow says. Kenny ignores him. He looks at the licenses, looks at us, and shrugs. Cassie hands them back to us.

"Thank you," I say, trying to compensate for the fact Minnow is glaring. I want her to like me, as if it matters. Maybe it's because she seems so average, so unaware of the horrible parts of life, like the girls in high school who said nice things to me when I came back to class after my father's funeral. I was seventeen when my mother found my father's body in the garage, the gun he had bought years back, after two break-ins on our street, at his side. After that, my mother and I could not look at each other without feeling we should have done something to prevent it. My father had been sick since I was young, on and off different meds that made him fall asleep at the dinner table and kept him up watching old movies all night. I was used to him that way. In the weeks before he died, I had thought he was getting better, again; he'd started lifting weights in the basement and telling us stories about his college days in Orono when he played hockey for the Black Bears. In actuality, he was off his meds. At school, I knew the girls speculated about what had pushed him over the edge, about whether it was my countless boyfriends or my mom's overnight shifts, or if maybe we wanted him to do it for the life insurance. In my new life, I realize I can't blame them for asking if it was my fault. I've asked myself the same thing a million times. In another world, those girls would have been my best friends. Maybe Cassie is not so different from me. Maybe she wishes things had turned out differently for her. Maybe she failed out of college, too, and there's nothing else for her to do.

Minnow orders a pitcher of beer and a double portion of the fried veggie basket. When Cassie brings out our order, the food is resting on deli paper on top of fake Easter basket grass. "Would you look at that presentation," Minnow says as she sets it down. "A-plus for effort."

"It's nice," I say. I want her to know that Minnow and I are in love, that things aren't as bad as they look.

Minnow puts a fried mushroom into his mouth and follows it with a long drink of beer. I tell him I am going to clean up. In the bathroom, I stand in front of the mirror, holding my bag, feeling as if I could be in any restaurant bathroom in any town, as if there's no reason for anything. I need to hear my mother's voice. I take out my phone and find her contact and press call, unsure what I will actually say. The phone rings four times, then stops.

"Where are you?" my mother asks.

"I don't know," I say. "Illinois."

"Oh, Michelle."

"It's okay, Mom, I'm fine. We're fine. We're working, doing stuff. We're driving to Maine."

Silence. Then, "So you're still with the Jenkins boy."

"Minnow."

Silence again. I know my mother is pinching her ear lobe, standing with one foot on top of the other and leaning her head on the kitchen wall, against the butterfly wallpaper I helped her put up.

"It's alright, Mom. We're fine."

She clears her throat. "Minnow. Such a strange name."

"Mom." I feel so tired. I squat, dizzy. I don't know why I thought calling my mother was a good idea anyway.

"I just wanted you to know that I'm okay."

"Are you coming home?"

"No. I can't. Not now. I told you we're going to Maine. We have jobs there. I'll make some money."

Seconds pass. I know this call is over, but I don't want to hang up.

"Michelle," my mother says finally. "I won't tell you this again. You can't save that boy. Nobody can, that's not how it works. You can't fix people just by loving them. I wish you could. I do."

"Yeah, I know."

"Do you?"

I think of Minnow at our table, alone, and realize I've spent too long in the bathroom. "Mom, I better go."

"Michelle." I hear her breath flutter and I know she is holding back a sob. "Is this how you want to live?"

I stand up, my head tingling a bit. "Yes," I say.

"Well, then. Alright. Please don't call again. I love you, but I can't do it anymore. I can't do this. You have to understand."

I press end without saying good-bye and bury my phone back in the bottom of my bag.

"You get lost?" Minnow asks as I sit back down. He has finished most of the fried veggies and half the beer and is lounging against the booth, his shirt now completely unbuttoned. More people are in the restaurant, families with kids in those wooden highchairs that every restaurant has, and I realize it is a Saturday night.

My mother's words hang in my mind, but I smile and ignore Minnow's sarcasm. "It feels weird to sit down and eat at a real table," I say, trying not to scratch at the bites on my belly. If we were detasseling, we'd be eating peanut butter and banana sandwiches out of the back of a pickup, covered in mud and unnamed pesticides that we had to sign a release form to work around.

Minnow sits up straight. His eyes shine. "I know," he says. "That's why this kind of life is good for us, Shell. Don't you see? We're living now, really living." He pushes the food toward me and pours more beer into his glass. "I mean, what was the last show you watched? When was the last time you stayed in bed all day, scrolling through pictures of other peoples' lives?"

I can remember the last show I watched. Law and Order on Minnow's Hulu account back in Massachusetts, the night before we left for Nebraska. I remember because my mom and I always used to watch Law and Order and do the crossword puzzle together. She would start on the Acrosses until an ad came on, and then we'd switch and I'd do the Downs.

"It feels like a long time ago," I say.

Minnow picks at his sunburn. "I could do this until I die. I don't ever want to go back, do you?"

I don't even know if I can go back.

"I mean, Shell, I don't think about *them* anymore. Do you," he pauses, leans across the table toward me. "Do you think about your dad out here?"

"No," I say, wanting it to be true.

Minnow nods. "And berries will be better. That's what everyone says. I got us into a good crew, too, with Wyman's, and the crop should be good this year. And in Maine there are lakes everywhere, crystal clear water you can drink. We can go swimming every day."

Is that what I want? I don't know, maybe it is. All I can think to say is, "And you'll keep taking your meds?"

"What? Oh, well, yeah. You know I will. If that's what Nurse Shell wants." Minnow winks.

I let my mother's sadness drop away. As long as Minnow is okay, I know things will work out. "We'll swim in lakes?"

"Work in the fields, swim in the lakes, sleep on the ground. It's so simple, so beautiful. And after berries, we'll do apples in Wisconsin. And then oranges in Florida. Grapes in Virginia. We can keep going like this, as long as we want. Fucking forever."

Minnow says the last part too loud, and the other customers turn and look at us. I feel self-conscious, but then I catch Cassie's eyes across the room and I don't blink, I look straight at her and dare her to look away. Minnow pours the rest of the pitcher into my glass and signals Cassie. She takes her time coming over and keeps looking back at Kenny.

"Another one," Minnow says. He picks up the empty pitcher.

Cassie sets down our bill. "Folks are gonna need this booth," she says, softly. "I can't serve you unless you order more food."

Minnow slams the pitcher against the table. "Well actually you can," he says. "We're paying customers just like everyone else."

"Let's go," I whisper. I know we're not the kind of people they want in their restaurant.

Minnow's eyes water and he blinks. "No. That's unacceptable," he says. I reach across the table and put my hand on his arm, but he shakes me off and grabs the veggie basket and throws it on the floor. Easter basket grass goes everywhere. I want to remind him about the principle, but instead I stand up and walk toward the mess, bending to clean it up, and then I hear something shatter and see shards of beer glass skitter across the floor. People are gasping and Kenny is coming toward us. When I look back, Minnow is throwing the other beer glass on the floor, too. I lunge to grab it from his hand, but I'm too late and it shatters in front of my foot, sending a quarter sized shard of glass into the back of my ankle. Kenny reaches for Minnow's shoulder, and I throw my arms around Minnow and pull him outside, Kenny yelling about calling the cops. At first, the Bentley won't start. Minnow turns the key and nothing happens and his hand on the wheel is shaking. Neither of us speak, but then after another try the engine comes to life. Minnow punches the ceiling and speeds out of the lot. Cassie is standing in the open door, watching us leave with her sad apple eyes.

We get back on the highway, and Minnow rants for several minutes about ignorance and shallowness and how nobody would treat us that way if they knew who he was, how much money was in his bank account. When Minnow quiets, I hold my breath and pull the glass out of my ankle. All at once, the blood comes. Blood drips on the carpet. I start to feel faint and reach back to grab one of Minnow's dirty T-shirts, and I tell Minnow that I need him to find us a hotel for the night, no more driving. I pull my leg up to my chest, resting my foot on the seat, and press the T-shirt onto my ankle. Minnow doesn't even notice at first. When he looks over, the shadows of his face grow long in the shine of oncoming headlights.

"I did that, didn't I," he says. I don't answer.

"Fuck, Shell." Minnow pushes the hair back from his eyes and starts to cry. I haven't seen him do this before. He grits his teeth together and sucks breath through his mouth.

Off the next exit, we find a Holiday Inn. Minnow wipes his face on his shirt and grabs a credit card from the glove compartment and goes into the lobby. I wait in the car and take deep breaths and hope for the bleeding to stop. When Minnow comes back out, we each gather a handful of clothes and head to the second floor, and I am so relieved to be in a real room again, with a real bathtub and toilet and soft bed where chiggers can't burrow into my skin while I sleep, that my mood softens a little and I try to forget what we've just been through. Minnow seems to relax, too. While I take a shower and wrap toilet paper around my ankle, Minnow lies on the bed, his knees pulled up to his chest. I cover myself with a towel and sit next to him, and he moves his head into my lap.

"I drank too much," he says.

"It doesn't matter," I say.

"I'm sorry."

"They shouldn't have treated us like that. At least we got out of there before the police showed up."

"I didn't mean to hurt you, Shell."

"No. I know."

"I won't do it again."

I pat Minnow's hair. I think of how many times Minnow has said he won't do something again—won't drink, won't fight, won't spit out his meds. Each time, I believe him.

He sniffs and uses my towel to wipe his nose. "We're still going to Maine, right?"

"Yes."

"They've got lakes."

"I love to swim."

Minnow raises himself from my lap and smiles with his jagged tooth. I let him push me back onto the bed. He kisses me on the lips and neck, and I can feel the tips of his hair on my closed eyelids, the starchy familiarity comforting. His body is shaky on top of mine, fragile. Minnow kicks off his skirt. It's been weeks since we've been alone like this, away from the other workers in their tents. I reach down and touch him, expecting to find what I always find, but this time is different. At first I am happy, excited that this will happen after so long, that maybe everything from tonight can be wiped away with an act of love. And then I realize what it means. Minnow's lies repeat in my ears on a loop. *Anything for you, Nurse Shell.*

Our movements are hurried, breathless. Afterwards, Minnow rolls away and sleeps, naked on top of the comforter. I get up. There are blood stains on the blanket. The toilet paper has fallen off, but soggy bits still stick to my ankle. I worry that the bleeding won't stop, won't ever clot. I worry there's something wrong with me. I tap Minnow, wanting him to wake up and get me some bandages. But he doesn't stir.

Even though I know I shouldn't, I dig out my phone and pull up my mother's number. The battery icon is a red sliver. I want to ask her about my ankle. She knows about stuff like that, she'll probably tell me that I'm fine, I'm overreacting, that it's just a stupid cut. The phone rings and each time I wait for the pause, for the voice on the other end to say, "Michelle. I thought I told you not to call." When it goes to voicemail, I hang up, and then I try again, letting it ring until the voicemail message comes on again. She must be asleep, I tell myself. It's late, after eleven. But I don't believe it, and I know I am alone. I start feeling really scared, maybe for the first time in this new life. I want Band-Aids, I decide—real ones, not duct tape or toilet paper. After one last attempt to wake Minnow, I wrap more toilet paper around my ankle, take the keys to the Bentley from on top of the TV and slip out of the room.

Outside, the night is warm and heavy. I unlock the door and slide into the driver's seat. I have to adjust it so that my legs can reach the pedals. I don't know where a drugstore would be, or if one would even be open at this hour. If Minnow wakes up and sees the keys are gone, he'll kill me, but I'm no longer worried about that.

 I drive slowly through the parking lot, twisting knobs until the headlights come on, accidentally turning on the wipers. I've driven my mother's VW lots of times, though I've never owned my own car. Driving the Bentley feels good. I take a right onto the road and drive toward what looks to be the lights of a town. On both sides of me, wheat fields stretch out in the moonlight, and I press harder on the gas pedal and ease the Bentley up to speed. I turn on the radio and light a clove, and the edges of my fear melt into a calm that feels almost like hope. The Bentley's steering wheel vibrates as the car accelerates, my toes pressing down on the pedal, my mind humming with movement. As I hit sixty miles per hour, I realize I don't want to stop. I don't want to go back. The gas tank is almost full. I wonder, how far could I get?

 Up ahead I see a Walgreens, lit up inside. I slow down and turn in, bringing the Bentley to a stop in the empty parking lot in front of the store. I twist the key and the engine quiets. I take one last drag on the clove and flick it through the window, then grab my bag and push open the Bentley's door. At the glass entryway, I realize no one is inside; the lights are on, but dimmed, and the automatic doors are locked. My chest tightens because my ankle is throbbing, again, and the cut has reopened. I take my phone out of my bag, press the home button several times, but the screen remains black. For a while, I stand there, holding my dead phone, wishing there was someone inside who might see me and let me in. I gaze at the cash register, the newspaper rack, the tower of batteries by the first aisle. So close. And then, in a wash of relief, I realize I can drive to the next Walgreens, and if that one's closed, I'll drive to the one after that. Eventually, someone has to help me. I go back to the Bentley and climb inside, ease onto the soft leather seat, careful of my ankle. One more fresh start. All I have to do is drive.

I press the brake and turn the key, but nothing happens. The dashboard is dark, the key simply clicks. I pull the key out and blow on it with hot breath, as I've seen Minnow do, and then I put it back in. *Please*, I think. I'm only asking for one more chance. I turn the key again, and then another time. Still, the car does not start. I hold my breath and count to ten, staring through the windshield. The parking lot is dark, and beside it, the road is long and silent. No one is coming to save me. But what can I do? I try the key again. I try again. I try again.

The Visit

On his stepbrother's fourth day in the hospital, Owen came. He left his laptop and the pack of cigarettes he was trying not to smoke in his car, and feeling empty handed, he stopped at the Dunkin Donuts next to Radiology and bought a box of donut holes from a girl who reminded him of his daughter.

Bobby's size-fourteen feet poked out of the blanket, hospital socks stretching at his heels. An IV was thickly taped over the back of his hand. "I made it," Owen said, miming a forehead wipe as if he had jogged and not driven the hundred miles from his condo near the coast. The case worker, whose name Owen probably should have remembered from the call he received last week, snapped her gum and gathered the sweatshirt from the chair, stuffing it into a reusable grocery bag.

"Bobby," she said. "Your brother is here."

"*Step*brother," Owen corrected, the words out of his mouth before he could stop them. He had come to the hospital with the hope of becoming a better person, though upon seeing the network of tubing and fluid filled bags hanging behind Bobby's bed, that resolve was quickly draining from him. Owen was not good with suffering, or need, or much of what his ex-wife, Sara, referred to as the *human element*. He had not seen Bobby since Owen's mother's funeral, which had followed Bobby's father's funeral, nearly ten years ago. Owen's daughter was a teenager, then, her difficult habits just beginning. She had come with Owen because it fell on his one weekend a month of custody. Owen recalled her blowing her nose noisily during the service and when he turned to give her a look of exasperation, he had realized that she was, in fact, crying. His own eyes had remained dry.

"Hey, Bob-o. It's Owen." He looked for a spot to set the donuts.

"I know you, don't I?" Bobby said.

After their parents died, Owen had been relieved to find the arrangements for Bobby's care had been made in advance and none of them involved him. Bobby was put into a state-run home for the intellectually disabled. While Owen sent donations to the home and asked his secretary to source size-fourteen Velcro sneakers so Bobby would never go without, he had not visited Bobby there.

"I heard about your operation. How're you feeling? All better?"

The woman stared at Owen, and this time, Owen bit his tongue. *Relax lady, I know he's a goner,* he might've said. It came from the part of him that seemed to tangle up emotions with punchlines when the stakes were high. What had been his reaction when the neurologist informed Owen and Sara that their daughter would likely never speak again? He'd laughed. Laughed! Not a hee-hee but a solid, whacking ha!, while Sara's head went to her knees. He had never been more devastated, but there it was, that guttural sound as if he were pointing a finger at a mirror: gotcha, buddy.

"You'll need to watch him with that IV," the woman said, and suddenly Owen realized he was going to be left alone with Bobby.

Owen cleared his throat. "Oh, I'm sorry, but actually—" The woman threw her hand in the air without looking back. Owen began to sweat. He considered going after her.

"It's always something, isn't it," Bobby said.
"Sure is, Bob."

Bobby's room was the color of Pepto-Bismol, one wall patched with spackle that was left unpainted. A metal tray table with a plastic cup and straw, and what appeared to be the remains of orange Jell-O, had been rolled to the side of the bed. Owen wanted a cigarette. It was the first pack he had bought in six days, still wrapped in cellophane. When he was married, he snuck cigarettes here and there like a teenager, Sara's nose keen enough to pick up the scent even hours later, and still she nagged at him to quit, and still he told her that he had, almost. He moved to the chair beside the bed and sat, holding the donut box on his lap, certain that someone in full mastery of their human element would know what to say, though he did not. He pulled out his phone.

After a moment, Bobby asked "How's your car?"

"My car?" Owen looked up.

"Is it still in the shop?" Bobby asked.

Owen realized that Bobby did, in fact, recognize him, and was referring to the time when Owen wrapped his car around a tree thirty years prior, just after college. It had been snowing, and Sara, his girlfriend, then, had broken both wrists against the dashboard, though Owen had been fine.

"That was a long time ago, Bob-o. I have a new car now. It's fast—an Audi. I'll take you for a ride sometime."

Bobby grinned, and Owen could hear the wheeze of his breaths. "You had to junk the old one." Bobby slapped his palms together and twisted them, in a gesture that replicated the scrap metal crusher at the landfill Bobby loved going to see as a child.

"Yeah, Bob. Junked it." Owen watched a silverfish crawl out of a corner on the linoleum floor and move toward him.

"You're a dad now. No more funny business."

Yes, he was a dad. So, Bobby remembered that part, as well. His daughter and Bobby had been a natural pair when she was younger and their developmental stages had coincided. As she became an adolescent, though, she had grown quiet and distant, and on the rare occasions she agreed to join Owen on a visit to his parents' house, she would spend the hours curled into herself on the edge of the couch staring at her phone. Bobby would try asking her the same question over and over—How are you doing today? How are you doing?—hoping to win her attention. Every so often, out of kindness or annoyance Owen didn't know, his daughter would look up and say "I'm fine, Bob, thanks," meeting Bobby's eyes just long enough to appear sincere. And how Bobby's face would light up, just like that, again and again.

The silverfish skittered as if gliding on air.

Bobby sat up. "Did she come?"

Owen stepped on the silverfish, but not hard enough. The insect crept away. "Who?" As if he didn't know.

Julia. His daughter. After the incident, he and Sara had believed she would die. The tip of her skull above her forehead was shattered and a chunk of her brain was missing. The coma lasted eight days and on day six Owen called a funeral home and began to make arrangements, because that was what the doctor told him to do. When she didn't die, Owen felt a gratitude that weakened his knees, because it meant she would get better. Except that didn't happen either.

Now she wore diapers at night and needed her meals chopped into bits so she wouldn't choke, and she could not speak in words, only their shapeless approximations. Owen had not seen his daughter since she first woke up from her coma. Though there were tubes down her throat and she could barely open her eyes, he had sworn she stared right into him, imploringly, and it chilled him. He did not go to the rehabilitation center where she learned to maneuver a wheelchair and sign the words for "bathroom" and "drink," and he had not yet visited her since she had come home to Sara's house. Weekly, he called Sara, listening to her reports of seeing something like a smile on Julia's mouth when the cat nudged her leg, claims of hearing something like a laugh while the two of them watched reruns of Julia's favorite shows. Each conversation ended with Sara reminding Owen that he needed to visit his daughter, her flat tone suggesting it would be hard for Owen to become even more of a disappointment than he already was, but she was bracing for the possibility. What if Owen's face could unlock the frozen part of Julia's brain? Soon, Owen promised each time, citing meetings and sales conventions and now, Bobby. The truth was, he had tried. Twice, Owen had gotten as far as the highway exit of Sara's town. The last time he tried, he made it to the end of Sara's street, where he pulled over beneath a bony oak and called Sara to tell her something had come up. "You don't have to be afraid," Sara said. "She's different, but she's still Julia." But that's what Owen feared, that Julia would still be there, behind her slack face, knowing he had not saved her.

"She couldn't come," Owen said, but he brought up a photo on his phone and showed it to Bobby. The picture had been taken on Julia's twenty-third birthday, during a small window of time in Julia's adult life when she was not disappearing for weeks at a time and then turning up at Owen's condo, needing a place to stay and money, always money. She had a job at a frame store and rented a room in an apartment with two other young women, which was an improvement over that converted garage where she'd stayed with a boyfriend and his brothers. The photo he showed Bobby was the only one he had. Sara had texted it to him. In it, Julia was gazing across the restaurant, her wild, red hair pulled into a crocheted headband. Owen had arrived late to that dinner, barely in time for cake, bringing a card with $2,000 cash. Julia's chin had quivered as her fingers slid over the bills, crisp and new from the teller. He had reached out a hand to squeeze her shoulder as he would have when she was small and was about to cry during the sad part of a movie, but then, instead, he pulled his fingers into a fist and rapped his knuckles on the table in front of her, drawing her eyes back to him. Don't blow it all in one place, kid, he'd said.

"Time flies, Owen."

"That it does, Bob-o."

Bobby's eyes went to the IV and he began to scratch at it, and unsure what else to do, Owen handed over the box of donuts, placing them on the tray table. "Here, Bob," he said.

Bobby put one donut hole into his mouth, and then another, quickly forgetting about the IV. Owen thought of the girl at the donut shop who looked like Julia, how tempting it was to let himself believe, for a moment, that the events from the past few months had not happened at all, that Julia was right there, whole and unharmed. It was the same way Owen felt after Julia's inpatient detox stint, when he stopped by the frame shop for no reason except to check up on her, to reassure himself that she was okay, though as an excuse he brought along a bundle of Julia's junk mail that had been delivered to his condo. She had been too busy with customers to notice him, but there she was, perfectly fine. He left without a word, trembling from relief, dropping the mail into a trash can on the corner.

Bobby coughed, spraying donut crumbs onto the blanket.

"Hey, you okay?" Owen asked. Bobby coughed again, this time nearly retching. Owen pushed the plastic cup toward Bobby. Bobby opened his mouth and leaned in and Owen froze, realizing what Bobby was expecting him to do. He glanced at the door and willed a nurse to enter, but none did. Frowning, Owen held the straw to Bobby's lips and Bobby drank, pulling hard enough that Owen could feel the thrust of water in his fingers. The act felt oddly intimate, so much that Owen had to look away. When Bobby finished, Owen dumped the remaining donuts into the trash and pushed the box down to the bottom of the bin. What had he been thinking, bringing donuts to a dying man? It was a pointless gesture, like bringing tulips to Julia's hospital room when all they did was drop their petals and leave a mess.

Bobby fell back against his pillows and slept. Owen paced, fighting the urge to go outside and smoke. He walked to the window and stared out onto the parking lot, and beyond to where the ocean was waiting, at the end of the highway. What was he supposed to do? He had thought coming to the hospital would be one good thing and that, perhaps, other good things would then follow, and like crumbs dropped in the forest, those good things would form a path that led back to his daughter. He imagined the conversation he'd have with Sara that evening when he called to check in: *In the hospital with Bobby, no it doesn't look good, guessing I'll be here through the weekend, but how about I come by sometime next week, alright?* He'd say it, and he'd want it to be true.

The last time Owen saw Julia before the incident, he had stopped by her apartment to drop off a check to unclog her kitchen sink. Another problem, another check. Sara didn't approve, but she didn't stop him; she had no better ideas, herself. Julia had lost her job at the frame store and nobody was hiring. Owen knew it had to end, eventually, this handing over of money, no questions asked, but it was like quitting smoking—an event forever poised in the future, when conditions might be more favorable. When Julia opened the door, she was wearing a vintage REM T-shirt that fell over one bony shoulder and white tube socks that went to her knees. She stretched an arm across the doorframe, as if to block him. Peering behind her, Owen could see several garbage bags tied up and leaning against the fridge. "Are you going to let me in?" Owen asked, though he didn't want to go in—he was on his way back to the office, anyway, and had no intentions of staying—but he wanted to be asked. When he saw her hesitation, her darting stare, Owen felt a sinking in his chest. He shook his head. "Okay, kid," Owen said, pulling out his checkbook.

What would have happened if he had gone in? Would it have made a difference? Owen was already running late. He provided the requested sum, even going so far as to ask the plumber's name as he made out the check against the back of the door. "Thanks, Daddy," Julia said, the creases of her brow softening as the check moved from Owen's hand into hers, and Owen saw this was what their relationship had become.

The next day, when his phone vibrated and Julia's name appeared on the screen, Owen assumed it was because the plumber required more money. Owen was closing the biggest deal of the year, an account he'd spent months chasing. If he remembered correctly, Owen might have felt irritated by his daughter's call, a twitch of annoyance, perhaps even more. His face might have flushed just slightly as he removed his phone from the desk and pressed decline and dropped the phone into his case, and in his head he might have said "for fuck's sake, Julia," and might have planned to say it to her, later, as he wrote out another check from his endless supply of checks. Regardless, Owen closed the deal with a smile on his face, shook hands, made a joke or two about the weather, and by the time he got into his Audi and checked his voicemail, Julia had been shot.

Bobby jolted awake. "I have to pee."

"Christ. Hold on." Owen's eyes jumped from Bobby to the IV stand as he tried to figure out what to unplug to free Bobby so he could get to the bathroom.

"I'm done."

Owen saw the wetness spreading through the blanket. "Christ," he repeated, pressing the call button on the side of Bobby's bed.

Bobby shuddered. "It's always something."

"It's a mess, Bob," Owen said. "That's what it is."

Bobby looked at his groin. "I'm sorry."

Owen squeezed his eyes shut and rubbed his temples. Now, he needed a cigarette. "It's fine, Bob. It was an accident."

An accident. That's what the investigator kept coming back to, a deal gone astray. It was no secret drugs were involved, which seemed to cast a guilty shadow that made Julia somehow deserving of what happened to her. The shooter had not been apprehended and likely wouldn't be without Julia in a position to identify him. Sara wanted no part of it, she focused her energies on Julia, but Owen had been paying a private detective. So far, nothing had come to light.

Owen pressed the call button again, then glanced into the empty hallway. "Hey! Can we get a nurse in here?" Bobby winced as if he were in pain. He began rubbing his fingers over the IV on the back of his hand.

"Don't touch that," Owen said, but Bobby did not seem to hear. Again, Owen stuck his head into the hall. Turning back, he saw Bobby had peeled off an edge of the tape. Owen watched Bobby pick at it, and his jaw clenched. He had to get out of the room.

Around the first corner, Owen found a young nurse coming out of a room and pushing a vitals cart. Owen put a hand on the cart, stopping her, forcing her to listen to him. He felt as if he needed to make his case, that Bobby was disabled, and dying. And really, Owen shouldn't even be here in the first place. The whole idea that coming to see Bobby would make Owen better, make him more *human*, was flawed because Owen was exactly who he was. He was a man who was begging a nurse to touch his stepbrother's bedding so he didn't have to, a man who was probably not even going to go to the funeral to see Bobby laid out in his best suit and a shiny, new pair of size-fourteen Velcro sneakers. All Owen really wanted was to be in his car with the window cracked and a cigarette in his lips, driving away. "Room 314 needs a bed change," he said, instead.

"Give me a minute," the nurse said.

When Owen came back to the room, the blanket over Bobby was sprayed with blood. There was a smear of blood on the back of Bobby's hand, where the IV had been pulled out, and splatters on Bobby's cheek. Owen felt the paralysis of indecision, the same way he had felt when he listened to Julia's voicemail in his car after the meeting, hearing her lowered voice, the way she whispered *Daddy, I need help.* What had she thought would happen? Even if he had taken the call, he would not have had time to get to her apartment, to whisk her away from the bullet. He was not Superman; he had no superpowers. But she thought he did, and that was the thing. That was the thing.

"You know better, Bob-o." Blood was everywhere. Owen was dizzy. He leaned back against the wall, feeling a fuzziness behind his eyes.

"I don't like needles," Bobby said.

The nurse entered. Without a word, she put on gloves.

Owen pressed the back of his head into the wall. He looked away while the nurse cleaned Bobby and set the pile of bloodied wipes on the tray table that had once held donuts. She opened the cupboard behind the bed to get a new IV needle. Owen knew he ought to warn her, but he just wanted it to be over. "Alright, now," she said. "A little pinch."

Immediately, Bobby punched. His fist hit the underside of the tray and sent the metal flying, crashing with an explosive bang. Bobby yelled in a voice Owen had not heard before, a high-pitched scream like that of a frightened child. "Don't!" Bobby cried, and a man in scrubs brushed past Owen to enter the room, and he and the nurse seemed to exchange some silent plan of action. While the nurse worked on Bobby's hand, the man forced Bobby down, pressing Bobby's linebacker shoulders into the mattress.

Owen could do nothing. He pushed his entire body into the wall.

Bobby kicked off the blanket, exposing his naked legs and the dampness between them. He cried long, rolling sobs and strained against the restraint. Bobby's cries came like waves, cresting and falling and then building again, assaulting Owen. Owen could feel the sound in his core, resonating, humming with his breaths. Was he crying, too? Owen wasn't certain anymore. It was all too much. Bobby was dying. Owen's daughter was gone. There was a sadness in this world that waited like a period at the end of a sentence, and Owen had reached it now, and he did not know if there would be anything beyond.

The nurse worked swiftly, placing the new IV, and when it was done, Bobby went limp. His wet eyes blinked. It was as if a storm had passed through the room and was gone.

No one noticed Owen leave.

He stepped into the elevator and pressed the first-floor button repeatedly until the doors closed. As the elevator jolted down, Owen pictured his cigarettes and his car and the highway that led back to the ocean, and he kneaded his hands to stop them from shaking. It was too late for Bobby. Nothing could be done about that. Owen would go and Bobby would forget he'd ever come, and Owen would try to be a better person tomorrow, or the next day. There was always another day.

Turning left out of the elevator, Owen broke into a jog, slowing only as he passed the Dunkin Donuts. The girl was still there, as she had been earlier, wearing her brown apron and cap. She looked so much like Julia. Owen paused there, catching his breath in the open doorway of the shop.

"Can I help you?" the girl asked.

Her voice, as well, so similar. Owen stood, taking her in. He would not come back to this hospital. He would not see Bobby, or this girl, again. And though he knew this girl was not Julia, he also knew this was his last moment of hoping she could be.

"Sir?"

Owen wanted to say something to her. He moved toward the register.

The girl waited.

Owen tallied up the shared traits—the wavy, red hair, small nose, the shoulders, though he couldn't make them out under the girl's brown uniform, that he knew would be delicate knobs of bone and skin, like Julia's.

"Sir?"

The girl's smile was failing. Owen tried to think of the right thing to say. Perhaps he should apologize for staring. Maybe he could show her the photo of Julia on his phone. Would she see the resemblance? He needed her to understand there was meaning here. There had to be.

The girl paused, and when he didn't respond, she rolled her eyes and turned her back. She busied herself cleaning the frother with a cup of water. Owen remained. He knew he ought to go, but the moment felt unfinished. He watched the girl's back, his mind blank. Finally, he pulled out his wallet and extracted a fifty, slipped it into the tip cup by the register, rapped his knuckles twice on the counter, and walked away before the girl turned around. He pushed through the hospital doors and out, into the brisk air, making his way to his car. His cigarettes were where he had left them on the passenger's seat. Turning the ignition, Owen pictured the girl's smile as she discovered the money he'd left, and the day seemed to brighten around him. It wasn't much, but she was young. She could use it. She was such a beautiful girl, with her whole life in front of her.

Dysfluency

The second he comes home I look for a sign. Auggie is my last child, the boy who once slept with his hand under my shirt rubbing the cluster of moles above my hip. A cowlick still lifts the shag of bleached hair over his forehead, a bloom of pimples darkens his jaw. He climbs out of his father's Tahoe dragging an overstuffed duffel bag behind him, legs spreading over the pocked ice I salted while I waited for them this morning. He squints up at me, no slant in his gaze. And I look. I look.

His father wants to hire a lawyer. Anybody would wonder. Look up the numbers; you're better off asking how many women it doesn't happen to. Those tender cheeked boys, the ones who sit in the front of the lecture hall, you think it's a joke, at first, how hard they press you down, their eyes on the wall, or anywhere but you. But there's always another side. I googled a lot of those accounts after I got the letter from Auggie's university suspending his room and board until the hearing. #MeToo run rampant, and the like. Boys whose lives have been derailed. Good boys, like Auggie. If you had asked me a month ago, I would have said goodness is no alibi. Now I feel like an atheist begging to be converted. Go ahead, convince me. Show me a sign.

The letter used the terms *alleged* and *misconduct* and *first year female*. Auggie won't tell me her name. He rarely speaks since coming home, though that's nothing new. Evenings, after I drive him back from class, he sits on his bed in his room with his gaming headphones on, picking up from where he left off this summer. The TV screen flashes with blood and zombies. If Auggie notices me parting his door so I can check on him, he doesn't let on. His face is intent on a battle that is only silence to me.

I WAS THIRTY-SEVEN when Auggie was born, my daughters already in school, my ex-husband, Ron, two years into an affair I had yet to discover. Eight months pregnant, I visited my dying grandmother. "A boy," she said to me, disapproval in her watery eyes. "A boy will grow up and leave, Lizzie. And what will you do?"

After the delivery, as if to drive home my grandmother's words, I was alone. Ron had left the hospital to care for the girls. My grandmother had died two days before. The nurse placed Auggie into my arms, his raisin face red from howling, and I thought—oh, it's *you*. I'd never tell my daughters, but Auggie was the only one I knew before he was born. I can't explain it. It was as if I had dreamt him into being, his body like a forgotten language. He didn't talk until he was three, but I knew what each cry meant, each frustrated grunt. At night, I could walk into his room and know from the thickness of his breath if he would wake up with a fever, or if he had been crying in the moment before he fell asleep.

Growing up, Auggie struggled in school and had few friends. His sisters were out of the house by the time he was eleven. He could go stretches without speaking more than one-word responses, though I could tell how his day had gone from the angle of his shoulders, the heaviness of his boots on the front steps. After the divorce, he developed an atypical stutter. He would repeat the word at the end of a sentence as if stalling for time. *I did my homework-work-work. I'm fine-ine-ine.* My heart broke for him, and yet I loved him more for it, as mothers do. Those cracks were how I got inside. How I knew him.

AUGGIE DOESN'T APPEAR DISTRESSED. He eats two bowls of Cinnamon Toast Crunch cereal in the morning, phone in hand, leaving a trail of brown flecked milk drips that I wipe up with the dish sponge. He puts off showers and instead douses himself in sandalwood-pine body spray that wafts through the house. The cat has gone back to sleeping in his tangled comforter during the day. I have gone back to imagining Auggie's days outside the house, moment by moment, as I did when he was in elementary school. Now he is opening his laptop and wiping the screen with his sleeve, now he is raising his hand. Do whispers follow him from class to class? Does he keep his eyes on the ground?

"Who is she?" I ask during dinner, as if the question has just popped into my head. I read once that, when surprised, people are more likely to answer honestly.

Auggie shrugs, raising the headphones around his neck. He eats quickly, carries his plate to the sink.

"You need to talk to me," I say, but he's gone back to his room. When he was eight, he was bullied on the bus and would come home with bruises on his shins, gum stuck to the back of his hair. He made excuses, but his stutter gave him away back then.

I watch him, waiting for a crack to open. At night, I stand by his door. The flicker of the TV lights the crack against the floorboards. The creaking of the bed, the click of trigger buttons on the video game controller tells me he is still awake. *Good night*, I say through the door, and I hold my breath, listening, in case this is the time he says it back.

SNOW BEGINS TO FALL while I park behind the science center and wait for Auggie to round the side of the brick building. It's a mid-tier school, close to home. His sisters had insisted on going out of state. *Boys grow up and leave*, I hear my grandmother say. But so far, Auggie stays.

Faces materialize, groups walking together. Boys in hoodies and Patriots hats and girls in leggings and fat boots, heads tilted to look at their phones. I scan the female bodies, wondering which one it could be, if I could tell just by looking. In my mind, she is small and fair, nervous, perhaps easily flustered. Is she a Catherine, or a Kaylee? Why it matters, I'm not sure. Except that she has something I don't have. She understands Auggie in a way I don't.

She knows what he's done.

There he is, trailing the group with two other boys. They are laughing. At first, I'm heartened to see him happy. With friends! Auggie is showing them something on his phone. One boy takes the phone and puts it close to his face and moves his mouth as if he is howling. Auggie looks behind and around him. He takes the phone back. The boy grabs again, and then the other boy reaches for the phone and Auggie presses it to his chest with his arms folded over and rolls into himself. I can't tell if it is meant to be a joke, this roughness between them. Or something more? The other boys don't turn when Auggie leaves them to come toward me. His head is down, moving in the direction of the car without looking at it.

"We got the date," I say, as he climbs in. I watch his face, which is flushed from the cold. He tosses his backpack onto the rear seat. I reverse from the spot and begin to drive.

"What?" he says. His eyebrows rise and fall. "Oh."

"Next Tuesday." One week away.

Auggie nods and wipes his phone on the thigh of his jeans, thumbs in the code.

"I thought we could practice," I say. Even on the slowest setting, the windshield wipers squeak, so I turn them on and off, on and off, giving the snow enough time to stick to the windshield before it is wiped away.

"Practice what?" He is scrolling.

"Your statement. What you're going to say to the board. They're going to ask questions. You have to be ready."

Auggie stops scrolling and smiles at something, then flicks it away with his thumb. "I'm just going to say what happened," he says.

"Of course," I say. I think of the boy from North Carolina who was expelled when he said hug, but she said grab. Was it because he said it with too much emotion? Or not enough? "But still, you should practice."

Auggie stares at his phone. Maybe he is reading, maybe the screen is black. "It's stupid," he says.

My chest burns. "What do you mean?"

"All of it. All of this, over nothing."

Wet flakes collect on the windshield and become transparent as they melt. My jaw flexes. I want to say: *then prove to me it's nothing.*

"Auggie," I say. "This is serious."

He is typing something, a text, but to whom?

"I know," he says.

"Do you?"

Auggie sniffs, wipes his nose with his sleeve. He looks out the window.

"Are you scared, honey?" I ask. His face is turned away from me. Another sniff.

"Because it's okay if you are. Anybody would be scared."

Auggie wipes his nose again. "Mom," he says, and the way he says it—*Mom*—softly and upturned, is just like the way he used to call out for me at night when he woke from a bad dream.

This is it, my crack. My way in. "What, honey?"

The windshield is patchy with drops and crystals, like looking through a prism. I want to tell Auggie that I will fix everything, if he will just open up to me. If he needs me to lie, I will lie; what else would a mother do? He's so close. I turn and touch his upper arm, rub the swishy fabric of his jacket. "You can tell me, it's okay." Auggie presses his eyes, says nothing. When I turn my gaze back to the road, the traffic light is a red blur through my windshield, and I brake too quickly. The car fishtails. Auggie bolts forward, one hand braced on the glove compartment. The car comes to a rest and we sit there, for a moment, breathing together, even after the light has changed. Then Auggie's phone dings, and he goes back to the screen. I turn on the wipers, and in one swoop everything becomes sharp.

AUGGIE GOES INTO HIS ROOM when we get home. I thaw chicken thighs in the sink. The light in the kitchen feels too bright, the sound of the cat crunching her food amplified in the silent space. The letter from the Dean is where I left it, on the island, refolded and fit back inside the opened envelope.

My phone trills. It is Auggie's father. I picture him, pulling closed the pocket doors to his den, in the oversized colonial he and Lana bought with her money, days after the divorce became final. Auggie was six. He thought his father lived in a castle. I answer as I always do. "Ronald," I say.

"Liz," he says. "I've got someone I want Auggie to speak with."

"A lawyer."

He clears his throat. "A friend of Lana's. Nothing official, Liz. Just someone to go over things with him. Before Tuesday."

I press my finger into the frozen chicken, feeling no give. I should have taken it out yesterday. "He doesn't need a lawyer," I say. "This isn't a criminal case."

Ron sighs. "I don't think that's the point, is it."

"What's the point, then?"

"To get our ducks in a row. To be prepared." His voice is clipped, irritated with me. When Auggie stuttered, Ron would say *come on now, spit it out.*

"You think he did it," I say.

"That's not what I said, Liz." Ron pauses, and I imagine him pacing with one hand on top of his head, the way he used to when he was on the phone with the bank. When we married, he wanted me to stay home. During the first few days of each month, when the bills were due, I knew to tiptoe around him.

"But who knows what the hell *she's* going to say," he says. "And who are they going to believe?"

For a moment I wait, ears pricked, as if expecting an answer.

WHEN DINNER IS READY, I knock on Auggie's door. I pause, knock again. Nothing. I open the door. The room is dark, the air heavy with the scent of dust from the radiators and unwashed clothes. Auggie is asleep on top of his covers, curled into a ball. One sneaker is on. He is holding his phone in his hand. I move closer, touching his forehead. He is breathing irregularly, long stretches in between each breath. He does not feel warm, but to be sure I lean down and touch my lips to his cheek. I can feel the beginnings of stubble, the raised acne scars. My mouth hovers there, above his skin, as if trying to absorb him into myself, to know him again. *I'm here*, I think. *Where are you?* I want to shake him. I want to tickle his armpits. I want to pick him up and throw him over my shoulder, anything for a response.

Just then, his phone lights up. A text bubble appears on the screen, half of it obscured by his thumb. My eyes prickle as they work to focus. The name *Pinkgrrl*. The words *pictures* and *police*. I reach for the phone. *Talk to me*, I want to type. *Please, tell me the truth*, though I'm terrified by what that might be. But as I pinch the glass and metal, Auggie inhales and rolls away, pulling the phone from my fingers.

The screen goes black, and I straighten up. There is no fever.

The next morning, he is in the same clothes. The strands of hair that fall over his eyes are darkened with oil, and he is standing in the kitchen with his backpack on. "I'm going to be late," he says.

I pour a cup of coffee and eye the phone in his hand. "Stay home today," I say.

"I can't."

"You don't look well." I want him to be sick. I want him to have the flu. Something to stop him in his tracks.

I stare at the phone, willing it to vibrate again, here where I can see Auggie's face, and he can see me watching. Auggie puts it into his back pocket. "I feel alright," he says. But the end of the word is drawn out, just slightly too long.

ALL DAY, I CANNOT SIT STILL. I put on a sweater and take it off again. I open my laptop and look up *Pinkgrrl* and Bridgeport State University. A list of social media accounts comes up. There is an image of a blond girl with cat ears, a vegan Instagram influencer, a Japanese YouTube channel. Where do I begin? I think about checking the phone records, but then I cannot make heads or tails of the options on the Verizon website. If this is the girl, and Auggie has pictures of her, I need to delete them. Maybe I should cancel Auggie's line altogether, erase everything. Sink the phone in an old can of paint in the basement. Except it's my only link to her. I need to know what she knows; I need her to tell me who my son is.

I want to scream at Auggie until he cracks. When he stuttered, I would pull his face to my chest and hold him there, until he was calm enough to speak clearly. Now, I might not be able to let go. I might hold him too tightly, cutting off airways. Bruising flesh. Snapping ribs.

Instead, I call Lana's lawyer friend.

I USED TO WISH MY GRANDMOTHER could see Auggie, somehow, from wherever she was, so she would understand there was no reason to feel sorry for me. A reverse séance. The living sending out a message to the dead: you don't have to worry, everything's okay here. I believed Auggie was different. More a part of me, somehow, as if our cells carried within them a memory of proximity. I knew him; therefore he was.

Now I am not sure.

I took him to a language pathologist for the stutter. She had a name for it, something clinical that I can't remember. Auggie hated the sessions. He would come out of her office holding back tears, though by the time we got to the car the tears would be gone, replaced with a sourness that verged on contempt. Still, the sessions worked. Auggie learned to sense when the stuttering was coming, and to relax into it, to release the tension rather than fight it. By ninth grade the stutter had resolved. He spoke less, but without hesitation. I didn't realize until it was too late that part of him had been sacrificed, the part of him he couldn't hide. The part that spoke directly to my heart. Auggie was never good with words, but without the stutter, we were both lost.

Sons grow up and leave. And what will you do?

Auggie is in the shower. The cat sits by the bathroom door. I pick a decent shirt from his closet, a lavender one with a stiff collar, and khakis with the tags still on them. A striped tie. He needs to look the part. Clothes and papers litter the floor of his room, but if I block them out his room looks the same as it did when he was twelve—the wrinkled world map poster over his bed, the cross-stitched brontosaurus with Auggie's name written in red thread across its back. A boy's room. Soon, I will drive him to the school's admissions building. The board members will be waiting. A decision will be made.

I think what scares me most is that I'll never know. We'll go on, Auggie will transfer schools, Ron will pay to have things forgotten, I'll scrape another winter's ice from my front steps, and I'll never really know. I'll lose him for good. Because how can I love him, if I can't know him? But then there's this thought: can I love him if he's guilty? Truly guilty? Perhaps that is actually what scares me most.

I set the clothes on Auggie's bed. The shower is still going. From under the mess of sheets, I hear a vibration, and without thinking, I dig for it. I burrow like a madwoman. I throw the sheets onto the floor and the phone hits with a thud, still vibrating. I pick it up. *Pinkgrrl.* The phone is alive in my hand. I swipe to take the call and put the phone to my ear. Someone is on the other end. I'm breathing too quickly; it's hard to think, and I know as soon as I speak she will probably hang up. "Please," I manage to say, because I don't know how else to begin. I expect the call to end—maybe I even want it to end—but it doesn't. The phone doesn't go dark. She stays on the line. She is there. She is listening. "I'm Auggie's mom," I say.

"Um, hi?" she says. Her voice is a girl's, small and young.

"Hi," I say. At once, the space between us closes.

And what will you do? What will you do?

Dinosaur

In the winter of 1991, Jude was fourteen, and the world was on fire. Jude watched smoke billowing from the oil fields in Kuwait on the evening news while she and her mother ate bowls of brown rice and vegetables on the couch. Iraqi troops had lit the fires during their retreat. "Senseless," Jude's mother said, as she always did, between bites of broccoli, her eyes rimmed red. Jude struggled to finish her meal, wondering where all that smoke would go.

"Your mom needs to lighten up," Cecilia told Jude. School was out, and they were walking to M&H Convenience, the only store this far out of town where Jude and Cecilia lived. Their boots were crunching over rutted ground that had thawed and refrozen in the errant arcs of tire tracks. They were looking for Tavi. It was Cecilia's idea to find the boy, to make him notice them, but Jude went along. Any time away from her mother was a relief, and Jude felt safe with Cecilia, insulated from her own worries under the blanket of her friend's chatter. Cecilia did not watch the news, did not think much about the war in the Middle East or the burning oil fields, but she knew things about how to be a woman that Jude did not know.

"She should put on some make-up and do her hair, for once. Show up at your dad's apartment in a Spandex dress and spike heels." Cecilia liked to come up with ways for

Jude's mother to get Jude's father back, each scheme involving provocative outfits that Jude's mother would never wear. Cecilia said women waxed the hair between their legs and wore bras and panties in matching colors, and that it was important to show a lot of enthusiasm when men kissed you, whether you liked it or not. Jude confessed that her mother wore men's button down shirts and cotton underwear with blood stains on the crotch, which she'd glimpsed, shamefully, when folding the laundry, and that she could not remember seeing her parents do anything more than dry pecks on the lips before her father's double shifts at the mill. "Well, there you have it," Cecilia had concluded. Cecilia suggested they make a list of reasons to hate Jude's father so Jude could let her anger out, but Jude didn't have any anger to let out. She didn't have any sadness, or any feelings at all, it seemed.

Cecilia leaned against the side of the store with one knee up, wiping her nose with a balled-up tissue, watching for Tavi. Jude scrunched her toes inside the black shapeless boots her mother had gotten half-priced at the Ames, probably from the boys' section. For a time, nobody came, no cars drove past. And then, walking up the middle of the empty road, Tavi came.

Jude and Cecilia knew Tavi as they knew all of the senior boys, as semi-celebrities, the rumors of their lives well circulated. Tavi was older, nineteen, since he lost most of his sophomore year because he was locked up at BMHI for suicidal tendencies. His actual name was Octavius, which sounded foreign, though his father, like everyone else's father, was from town and worked at the mill. Tavi wasn't attractive so much as he was compelling, in a tragic way. There were stories about him; one girl claimed he stood on the train tracks when a train was coming until she agreed to have sex with him. Other girls spoke his name as if it were a secret code, and that was how Jude and Cecilia imagined it: being chosen by Tavi equaled admission into a special group of girls who'd passed his test of desirability and were no longer nobodies.

Jude and Cecilia were freshmen. They had no other friends—Cecilia didn't because she had moved there in seventh grade to live with her grandmother, and Jude's reason was everyone knew about her father leaving, and because Jude's mother was not from Maine, and had no people there. When Cecilia was absent from school, Jude spent lunch in the fire escape stairway off the library. They had never been this close to Tavi before, though they had watched him from their school bus, his wool hat pulled down over his curls, smoking at the edge of the parking lot behind the school, towering over a ring of senior girls. It was Jude who came up with the nickname Dinosaur, when she saw the way Cecilia stared at Tavi, transfixed. Jude had been trying to make a joke of Tavi's lanky height, his neck so long she could picture him as a brontosaurus wading through a prehistoric bog, snatching limp weeds from beneath the water. "Yeah," Cecilia had agreed, her eyes still on the boy. "He's a T-Rex."

"Tavi," Cecilia called out. Jude startled. She hadn't thought Cecilia would dare to speak to him, not in real life. Slowly, as if it had been his intention the whole time, Tavi turned in their direction.

"Hi, there," Cecilia said. She uncrossed her arms, raised a hand, and wiggled her fingers in a gesture Jude had not seen her do before. "This is Judith, and I'm Cecilia," she said.

Tavi took them in, looking up and down. He didn't smile. "Pretty names for pretty faces."

"Thanks," Cecilia said, drawing the word out into two syllables.

A wind blew against the wooden store door, pulling it open enough to jingle the small bell above the door frame.

"Are you going in?" Tavi asked.

"We don't have any money." Cecilia curled her lips into a pout. She was acting like a different person. If Tavi hadn't been there, Jude would have punched Cecilia in the shoulder and told her to quit it.

"So, you're just going to stand here, then. In the cold." Tavi laughed.

"I don't mind the cold. Do you?" Cecilia smiled and locked eyes with Tavi, and for several moments the two stared at each other as if having a telepathic conversation. This felt like a game Jude didn't know how to play, like when her father would call to talk to her, and afterwards, her mother would ask questions that Jude tried to answer without making her mother cry, though her mother would cry anyway. Jude didn't cry. She wanted Tavi to look at her, too, and yet she was afraid to say a word.

"You have money, don't you?" Cecilia said, finally.

"Maybe I do."

"Well, you could grab us some gum."

"Could I?" Tavi half-grinned, revealing crooked canine teeth. He ran a hand over his hat, moving it back and forth, jostling his curls. "I'll see what I can do."

The bell on the door jingled as Tavi pulled it open, disappearing inside. The girls waited until it jingled again, and Tavi emerged, unwrapping the cellophane from a pack of Marlboros and tearing away the foil. He pulled one cigarette out, put it behind his ear, then reached into his back pocket and produced a pack of Juicy Fruit, which he tossed, winking, to Jude. Amazingly, she caught it. She didn't know if she should smile or say thank you or return the wink, so she did nothing, but the image of the wink stayed with her, replayed in her mind, and each time she imagined it, her insides throbbed. He had winked at her, not Cecilia.

As Tavi walked away, Cecilia took the gum from Jude and held it like a prize. "That was too easy," she said.

JUDE DID NOT TELL CECILIA she thought of Tavi over the next few days, or that she had inspected the M&H parking lot, looking for him, each time she rode past in her mother's car on the way to the grocery co-op. In her bedroom, while her mother was downstairs in front of the television, Jude pulled back the curtains on the large, plate glass windows that made up nearly one wall of her room. Once, her father was going to build her a balcony and put in sliders. The windows faced the small front yard and empty road and the surrounding woods that filled the half mile between Jude and Cecilia's houses, and at night the glass turned into a mirror, reflecting back the light of Jude's room. Jude stood there, watching herself, pretending Tavi was there looking back at her. She practiced tilting her head to one side, then the other, wiggling her fingers in a wave, the way Cecilia did.

Jude tugged her sweater over her head. She pulled down her jeans, kicking her legs free. She faced her reflection, trying to discern hints of a woman's body. Imagining what Cecilia would do, how she would move, Jude ran her fingers from her thighs up the sides of her body to the hollow of her armpits, then to the back of her head, pushing her hair up and letting it fall, strand by strand. She stretched and inhaled. It felt exciting, pretending to be someone else. As her hands fell back to her sides, she brought them down over her bra, feeling her nipples tingle. Then something hit against the window.

Jude dropped to the floor. She crawled to the window and cupped her hands to the glass to see outside, the only light out there coming from the lamp over the front door. Jude saw the shadowed figure of a tall boy who, as she watched, kicked at the frozen mud and picked up a chunk and threw it at her window. It looked like Tavi. Jude rolled away from the window. She stayed there, hugging the wall, very still except her racing breaths, until the thuds stopped.

The next day on the bus, Jude chewed her cheek while Cecilia went on about the fight she'd had with her grandmother.

"She wants me to walk the dogs because she's too fat to do it," Cecilia said. "But there's too many of them, all chained up out there. I wish they'd run away."

Jude thought of the boy outside her window. She was afraid to tell Cecilia, scared it would upset her, or make her angry because she would believe, as Jude did, that the boy was Tavi and now, as preposterous as it seemed, he had seen her naked. When Jude told Cecilia about spending the night at her father's new apartment in town, about the way his girlfriend—this one's name was Kat and she had shiny, fake nails that made her handle everything with the pads of her fingers—sat on her father's lap after dinner, Cecilia prank called his line from the pay phone outside M&H every day after school. "You're a sucky suckball," Cecilia said to the answering machine, trying to make her voice low and serious. Jude didn't tell Cecilia she had been there when her father played back his messages and deleted them one after another without even letting them play through. Her friend's voice sounded plain and undisguised on the recording. Jude had been in the next room, listening. It was just *"You're a suck—"* and then, beep. Her father had said nothing to Jude.

"Well? Am I boring you, as usual?" Cecilia asked.

"No, sorry," Jude said.

Cecilia withdrew the pack of gum from her pocket and ran her finger along the side. "Did I tell you I saw Tavi last night?"

Jude's face began to burn.

"I was feeding the dogs. He was walking from the direction of your house, up to M&H, I guess. I gave him a pack of Gram's Winstons. We sat on the back steps for a while." Cecilia sighed happily, as if sated. "Maybe he likes me. Do you think so?"

"I don't know." Jude let her bangs fall into her eyes. "Probably."

"He's so tall and weird. But he's cute, isn't he?"

Jude turned her head to the window. She didn't like the way Cecilia's voice changed when she talked about Tavi.

"Come on. You think he's cute, right?"

Through the foggy window, everything outside looked smoky and gray. It seemed only a matter of time before the oil fires would burn everything up. She wasn't sure why everyone wasn't more worried. Jude's mother had taken to watching the news with her head resting on the arm of the couch and a blanket up to her neck, which gave her a childlike look and made Jude feel as if she were on her own. "I just don't know," Jude said.

AFTER DINNER, JUDE WENT TO HER BEDROOM, again. She did not let herself look out the window, but she was waiting. She sat on her bed and waited. And then, thud.

Jude walked close to the windows, her body blocking enough light for her to see outside. The tall, male figure was down below. The boy raised his hand: hello. Jude's chest filled with the feeling she'd had before, when Tavi winked at her, and again when she'd first seen him at her window—a deep, hungry wanting. The boy pointed at her, then pretended to pull up his shirt. At first, Jude could not move. Again, the boy gestured. Jude thought of Cecilia and how surprised she would be to realize Tavi might actually like Jude, too, and she felt her body pull away from itself, felt the wanting in her chest take over. Jude slipped off her shirt and dropped it. The boy pointed to his pants. Jude took off her pants. Next, the boy raised his finger and twirled it. Jude wasn't sure what to do. Her skin prickled and heat rose to her face. Again, the boy twirled his finger. With sudden joy, Jude spun her body, relieved she had figured out the command. That she had done something right. Jude spun and spun.

When she stopped, Jude was sweating and warm and dizzy. Her hair settled over her breasts and her arms hung awkwardly at her sides. She stared at her reflection in the glass, afraid to look beyond it, out at the boy. As her dizziness cleared, her naked body appeared soft and girlish, once again, and she could not believe what she had just done. She reached down and picked up her shirt and held it to her chest. Slowly, she moved close to the window, blocking the inside light with her hand and squinting down at the boy, his face too dark to read. He lifted his hand again, and this time pointed his finger at her and curled it back to himself. Come here. Jude recognized the meaning immediately. Come to me, the way her father had gestured to Kat to sit on his lap after she cleared the dinner plates. But Jude didn't know how she could do that, how she could walk outside, naked as she was. How could she go to a boy whom Cecilia wanted for herself? Jude crawled to the wall and slid her hand over the light switch and waited there, in the dark, until the boy moved on.

Four days in a row, the boy came to Jude's window. He arrived after dinner, after the news with its pictures of oil lakes in the desert, of flames like rocket exhaust, enough smoke to fill the sky. Jude would go upstairs and stand in front of the window, curtains pulled back, until she heard the thud against the glass. She tried not to look down at him as she performed, though she knew he was there, which made looking into the reflection of her own face somehow thrilling. She knew the moves the boy would expect and she did them, improvising a little at a time, anything to keep him there. All day, she thought of the window time, what she would do that night, what the boy would like. How long he would stay, gazing up at her. For the first time since her father left, Jude found herself looking forward to something. She told herself that maybe the figure wasn't Tavi, maybe he was some other tall boy who liked to watch her, who liked her, the same way Tavi liked Cecilia, though she understood this was a lie. She understood Cecilia would be hurt if she knew, and it felt strange not to tell Cecilia, to have this between them, but it was the secrecy that made it real. Each night, Jude listened to her mother utter *senseless* at the news and wanted to tell her mother she was wrong—the fires weren't senseless, they were what happened when you wanted something so much you were willing to see it burn rather than let anyone else have it.

JUDE DECIDED SHE WOULD GO TO HIM, the tall boy, the next time he came to her window. If he returned, if he chose her over Cecilia, she would go to him when he signaled, outside into the dark and cold. She doubted her mother would even realize she'd gone. But the next night, the boy did not come. Jude waited until nine, then closed the curtains and went to bed. In the morning, waiting for the school bus with Cecilia, Jude shivered inside her jacket. Cecilia was unusually quiet, blowing her nose into tissue after tissue.

"Hey, look at this," Cecilia said, finally, shoving the used tissues into her pocket. She pulled her coat down around her neck, revealing a cluster of reddish-purple bruises.

"Did you get hurt?" Jude asked.

"No, silly. A boy did it, from kissing."

"Who was it?"

"Guess."

"No." Jude bit down hard on her cheek until she tasted iron. "Who was it?"

"Who do you think?"

Jude spread her feet for balance. She could smell something acrid in the air and wondered if the smoke from the oil fields had finally found them. "I don't know."

"Don't be dumb. You know."

Jude didn't want to say it. She held his name on her tongue, as if it would fly out and away from her if she opened her mouth. She didn't want to let him go.

"Fine." Cecilia rolled her eyes. "Tavi. It was Tavi. He came by when Gram went to bingo. I snuck him past the dogs by throwing them pepperoni." Cecilia sniffed and pulled one of the damp tissues from her pocket. She wiped hard at her nose. "He's pretty rough when he kisses," she said, looking down. The tissue was falling to pieces in Cecilia's fingers and she was trying to wad it back together. Once, her grandmother had made her go to school with a roll of toilet paper in her backpack because she had used up all the Kleenex in the house.

"You do think he's cute, though, don't you?" Cecilia asked. Her voice sounded shaky and Jude knew she was supposed to say yes. She was supposed to be Cecilia's friend. She was not supposed to be waiting, naked, by her window every night for Tavi. But Jude refused to be left behind, as her mother had been.

"I don't know. No. Not really." Jude felt it in her lungs, the smoke. It was thick. She coughed.

Cecilia straightened up and gazed down the road in the direction the bus would come. "Well, I like him. I do. You could probably get a boy to like you, too, if you tried a little, if you cared at all." She dropped the wasted tissue and it blew a few feet away. "You know, sometimes I don't think you care about anything." Jude remembered how Cecilia had let her stay over for a week last summer when her father moved out, how Cecilia had told her that parents don't even matter. Both of hers were dead, and she was just fine. Jude felt a surge of warmth from the memory, but she pushed it away. She thought of her father holding Kat on his lap. How her own mother would sometimes fall asleep on the couch and would still be there, breathing through her open mouth, when Jude got up in the morning. And she thought of the boy at her window, how he watched and watched, how she had seen him rub himself over his jeans and had felt both sickened and powerful.

"If you really want to know, I think he looks like a dinosaur," Jude said. "He's gross."

That night, Jude did not wait for Tavi to come. She walked to M&H, alone, saying Tavi's name over and over into the darkness. She didn't practice saying anything else, thinking if she could just say his name, it would be enough. At the convenience store, Jude went inside to warm up. She walked the aisles of canned goods and chips and maps and bottles of aspirin and shampoo. The store was hot and she began to sweat. She wished she didn't have her massive winter coat on and she unzipped it and alternated pulling one arm out at a time. Every few minutes she checked the front door to see if Tavi was coming.

The clerk watched her. "Hon, you need help or something?"

Jude picked out a candy bar and paid, flushing with heat. In the lot, Jude stood and chewed the sticky chocolate, feeling it melt in her hand. When she finished, she put the wrapper into her pocket and licked her fingers. She zipped her jacket back up. She waited. And then she saw him, coming up the road, his hands deep in his pockets and his shoulders hunched. He walked past her and into the store without slowing. Jude stepped closer to the light that spilled out of the store, just as the door shut and the bell jingled and Tavi went inside. She stayed there, in the middle of the unpaved, empty lot, so she would be in Tavi's path when he came out. He would have to see her. He would have to choose—her or Cecilia.

The door opened and Tavi came back out, hitting a pack of Marlboros upside down against his palm.

"Tavi," she called. Her voice was flat, but she'd done it. She'd said his name. Not like Cecilia, with her flirtatious flourish, but still, she had said it. Tavi opened the pack of cigarettes, dropping the cellophane on the ground, and pulled out two cigarettes, one for his mouth and one for behind his ear.

"Oh, hey. You need one?"

Jude met his eyes, searching for recognition. She wanted him to say her name, to remember. "No, thanks," she said. Tavi put up a hand to block the wind and lit his cigarette, taking a long drag that hollowed his cheeks. When he exhaled, smoke and vapor billowed in the air. Jude waited for him to say something about the things she had done in her window, for him to recall how she had shown him what he asked for and had moved her body in exactly the way he had instructed and that he had liked it, but he only smoked and looked away.

"Well, I'm here," she said, finally.

Tavi took another slow drag. He was watching the road.

"I came. Outside." Jude gestured at the parking lot as if to reinforce her point, then quickly pushed her hands into her pockets.

"So you did," Tavi said on his exhale.

Jude couldn't believe how close she was to Tavi. He was standing right there, talking to her, at least kind of. It made her feel bold. "You asked me to come, remember?" she said. "I was afraid, but I'm not anymore."

"Okay?" Tavi laughed, releasing the smoke in staccato puffs. "Congratulations, I guess."

She toed the hard mud. "I thought this was what you wanted," she said.

"What *I* wanted?" Tavi coughed into his fist and scanned the lot. He took a step away. "Look kid, I'm just here to get smokes."

Jude began to feel as if their window time had happened in another world far away from this one, or worse, not at all. "I mean, I know you like Cecilia, but still."

Tavi took a drag and blew the smoke over Jude's head. "Who?"

Jude wondered if he was joking, but she couldn't tell. There was an unreality to their interaction that was beginning to make Jude feel as if she were spinning. "She's the girl in the trailer with the dogs. You like her, don't you?"

Tavi looked away. "I don't know about that."

Jude's cheeks were hot. Suddenly she did not care who Tavi picked, whether it was her or Cecilia. She saw, now, that she and Cecilia were on the same side, could be the same person, in fact, and it didn't matter who Tavi chose, as long as they weren't both left behind.

"You do like her," Jude said, her eyes stinging. "Her name is Cecilia. You kissed her so hard it left bruises."

Tavi stepped back. "Hey, now," he said.

"You did. Don't you remember? Don't you remember Cecilia?" She took a step toward him and, again, he backed away. A pickup pulled into the lot and parked, the headlights briefly illuminating everything around them before shutting off.

"Who's Cecilia?" he said, and just the way it came out, with a shrug and darting eyes, made Jude understand that Tavi was embarrassed, she was embarrassing him with her presence, he was embarrassed to be caught there, at M&H, talking to her.

Jude was hot, flushing with sweat. Anger was rising in her. She was giddy with it. It consumed everything else—her hope that Tavi would like her, her jealousy, the numbness she held so close and the wanting that had broken through it. Her anger was burning everything up.

"She's my friend," Jude said, though she wasn't sure that was true, anymore.

"Fuck, kid. Who are you?"

Tavi flicked the butt of his cigarette over her shoulder and walked off, back down the road. Jude watched until he was gone. A man got out of the pickup truck and went past her, pausing for a second to nod politely, and into the store. Jude knew she should leave, but she could not bring herself to budge from her spot, to move from this moment into the next, into all the future moments that were to come. Standing there in the parking lot, she unzipped her coat and let the icy air blow it open, like wings at her sides. She knew if she was still there when the man came back out of the store, he would ask her if she was alright, if she was cold and needed a ride. He wouldn't be able to see the flames growing in her gut. He wouldn't realize that she was a fire, burning like oil, impossible to put out.

This Is How We Speak

For the third time this spring, Fonto calls to tell me she is dying. "Quinnie," she says, her mouth too close to the black cordless phone from the staff desk. I picture her quilted blue bathrobe, her prosthetic eyes glinting like marbles. "My belly hurts. Carrots are not my favorite. Nana Hickey is worried."

"Oh, Fonto," I say. It is after midnight and I am in bed, though I haven't slept. I rarely do, anymore. I sit up slowly so the mattress won't creak, a pointless habit. "Everything is fine."

"Can you come, Quinnie? I'm scared."

"You know I can't," I say. Beside me, Grant's half of the bed is tucked in. I go to the bathroom, turn on the light.

"Quinnie's having a baby," she says.

I shift the phone to my other hand and comb my hair with my fingers. My eyelids are puffy and a pillow crease runs across my cheek like an old scar. I tuck a streak of gray behind my ear. Fonto and I are the same age, forty-two, though she could pass for twenty-five, with her thick hair and unlined face and strong square teeth. We were neighbors growing up. My mother, who could not bear suffering of any kind, who cried the day a finch flew into the kitchen window and fell dead into her daffodils, made me walk Fonto home from school each day, and it embarrassed me, the way Fonto reached for

my hand at intersections, walked with her shoulder touching my arm, but I did it anyway. I took the longer route along the river where the other kids wouldn't see to save both of us from the teasing. "What color is ketchup," Fonto would ask in her raspy, low voice that should have belonged to anyone but her. "Blue?"
"Nope. Red."
"What happens if I eat too much ketchup?"
"You'll get a belly ache."
"Nana Hickey wears a Bam-Bam up-do."
"Uh-huh."
"I don't care for ketchup, do I, Quinnie."
"You prefer mustard."
"Can I have some mustard right now?"
"I'm fresh out, Fonto."

It was the same conversation every day, a script. Sometimes I'd give the wrong line to mess with her. "Ketchup is blue," I'd say, and she'd go silent for several minutes, swaying her head so her hair fell over her face. We'd walk a block before she would speak again. "It's red," she'd say, finally, her voice flat with disappointment.

"What's wrong with her eyeballs?" the girls at the pool would ask me, summers when Nana Hickey gave me ten dollars to take Fonto swimming for the day, though they knew, as everyone in town knew, that Fonto was born prematurely, that the oxygen in the incubator shrank her eyes to milky films in the backs of her sockets. They knew she had Down syndrome. They knew Fonto's mother had left her in the hospital when she was born to go drinking at the Blue Coyote and that she didn't come back, not the next day or any day after. They knew Nana Hickey was her mother, now, and if Nana Hickey were present, she would whack the back of their knees with her pocketbook for saying one word to Fonto. Just as they knew I would do nothing.

"Eyeballs? I'm fresh out," Fonto would say with a grin, revealing her unexpectedly perfect teeth. "Right, Quinnie?"

I pull my sweatpants down with one hand and sit on the toilet.

"I have to work in the morning," I say. I allow a small amount of urine to pass.

"You're tinkling," she says. "Nana Hickey says wipe front to back."

I lower the toilet lid without flushing. "Where's the staff, Fonto?"

"I don't know."

"You need to give the phone back. I'll see you on Friday." I've been doing it for twenty years, all through my marriage to Grant, first because my mother insisted, and then because I didn't know how to stop. It's always the same thing. We get mushroom pizza at Emma's and then drive around and listen to the radio until the streetlights come on. Sometimes we turn the music up so loud it hums in my ribs, and when the song ends, I feel cleaned out.

"Nana Hickey says I'm dying, Quinnie," she says. She begins to cry, which sounds like a clicking in her throat. I know her lips are making a big, silent circle, which always reminds me of a fish out of water, sucking useless breaths of air.

"Stop it, Fonto. Seriously."

Now she's singing. I can make out the chorus of "Africa," her voice wet and thick.

"Fonto, you hate that song."

She goes on singing.

"Cut it out," I say, trying to be louder than her song. "Go to bed. Get some rest." Just saying the word *rest* makes me realize how tired I am.

Her singing pauses. "Toto makes me cry, Quinnie."

"I know." I wet a face cloth with cold water and hold it over one eye while the song repeats in my head. The conversations

I have with Fonto do the same, her phrases ringing in my ears as I sit at a red light or boil water for rice. *Toto makes me cry, Nana Hickey wears a Bam-Bam up-do, carrots are not my favorite.* Occasionally her repertoire expands, like how she asks me about the baby, now. By the time she starts singing, it means she is past the point of being talked down, her voice quivering. Though Fonto's eyes are undeveloped, her lachrymal glands function normally, producing tears. If she cries without her prosthetics in, tears pool in the empty sockets and spill out in waves.

"Alright," I say. Even if I try, I will not sleep tonight. "I'm coming." I wait for her to finish her song, but Fonto is gone; the phone has been hung up.

IT'S ONE OF TWO TRUTHS I have never admitted to anyone: Katherine Fonto is my best friend. Like aging, it didn't happen overnight—for years, she was an embarrassment, then an obligation—but one day you look in the mirror and see a stranger and you realize, this is who I really am. Sometimes I think I should adopt her, become her legal guardian and take her out of the state-run home, known as Bright House, where she's been since she was twenty-three when Nana Hickey had a stroke and died. I could paint the empty second bedroom pink and put down a shaggy rug. Grant hated the idea, though his reasoning was sound enough, or at least I thought so at the time. He said we needed to focus on having our own children. He had already waited so long for me to be ready. And we were hardly rich, Grant being a middle school teacher and me at the bookstore that was always threatening to go out of business. Fonto was happy at the Home, he insisted.

"How can you be sure?" I asked, once, during the time I now look back on as the beginning of the end, just before we found out I was pregnant. I rarely questioned Grant. He had a way of arguing that seemed to tangle up my words and made me feel foolish for not being able to straighten them back out. "What makes you think she's happy?" I had just learned that Fonto had been put on a new medication, an antidepressant. It wasn't something I was supposed to know about, as I was not Fonto's guardian and therefore not involved in her medical care, but the staff gave me her eight o'clock meds each time I took her to Emma's, and when I poured them out onto a napkin, one night, I recognized the green capsule as Prozac because I was on it, too.

"Honestly, Quinn. I just mean she's being taken care of there." He raised his eyebrows in an effort to show he was being logical. "You don't need to worry about her." That was two years ago, in March, when the baby was an undetected bean inside me. We were in the kitchen that we had recently updated on a budget, Grant having spent his February vacation resurfacing the oak cabinets in an antique white. The room still held the hopeful scent of paint. I was chopping salad for dinner while Grant stood at the slider and gazed out at our muddy stamp of lawn. He put a hand on the glass and turned to me. "She spends her life listening to her Walkman and finger-painting at the day program. Would she even know the difference?"

I shivered with emotion. The one time I brought Grant with me to see Fonto, a year into our marriage, he stuck so close to me I worried he might try to follow when I took Fonto into the bathroom to help her shower. Afterwards, he said it wasn't Fonto, but the place itself that had made him uncomfortable. It was the smell, which I had gotten used to, the scent of bleach and urine and, often, feces, though the staff did their best to keep the large house clean and inviting, putting seasonal placemats on the table and photo collages of the residents on poster boards in the hall. It was the heat, set at a medicinal eighty. It was the residents. There were five, not including Fonto, and some had lived there as long as she had, becoming a familiar backdrop to my visits.

I knew Phil would ask about the condition of my car, and when Larry said "chocolate éclair" it meant he was going to hit someone. Grant explained that it was unnerving for him, not being familiar with everyone, not knowing how to act around them. He seemed to find Fonto and the other residents inscrutable, regarding them with an expression of guarded pity, as if they were speaking a language he didn't know and couldn't possibly be expected to understand.

"I know you mean well," Grant said that day in the kitchen, walking to the island where I was slicing olives. I stared at the fingerprints he'd left on the glass. "But Fonto's not your responsibility."

Of course she is, I didn't say.

Every time I left Bright House, part of me believed I'd never return, that I could walk away for good. But each Friday, I went back. That was something I could not make Grant see: the duty we have to each other, whether we want it or not.

When my ultrasound, and subsequent blood tests, revealed abnormalities, Grant agreed that we should follow the doctor's recommendation and terminate. He said we would try again, and I think he believed it, though I was already forty, and we both knew these defects had a low, but definite probability of recurring. For years I had been afraid of having a child who would need too much from me, the way Fonto did. Now that it was happening, I felt under the weight of a boulder and I wanted to run away from my own body.

I was eighteen weeks along at the time of the procedure. The baby was a girl. Coming home, I could not speak, and Grant turned the radio to NPR, letting someone else's words fill up the space. He preferred we not tell friends and family; he'd called the bookstore for me and said I had the stomach flu. But I had already told Fonto of the pregnancy, and after it was over she continued to talk about it. The words hurt, and then they didn't, the way pain can turn to pleasure when you stop fighting it.

"Quinnie is having a baby," she would say.

"Yes," I'd say. "A girl."

"When will she come?"

"Not for a while."

"After the Fourth of July?"

"Yes."

"I don't care for waiting, do I."

"Nobody does, Fonto."

"We'll have the baby soon, Quinnie. She'll be a girl."

Hearing those words was a refuge for me, one I came back to over and over. I knew it wasn't right. I knew I should make Fonto understand the baby was gone, but I didn't. Friday after Friday, Fonto and I spoke about the baby, whose birth was always put off beyond the next holiday. After Thanksgiving. After Christmas. After. It didn't matter to Fonto that more than nine months had passed. Time, to Fonto, was a swimming pool she could bob in with her foam swim collar; every direction felt the same until she bumped into something solid. I could go on telling her I was pregnant, and she would go on believing it until I pressed her palm to my flat belly and told her the baby had left us both.

Grant refused to speak of what we had done. "It's morbid, Quinn," he said, frustrated that I would not consider becoming pregnant again, despite the doctor's warning I was running out of time. "You need to let it go. Get back into life." Grant did both of these things with no perceivable trouble. He joined an adult softball league and took a "Learn to Speak Italian" class at the adult education center which seemed to run later and later each week. He moved on. He moved away from me a little each day until he was gone.

The other truth I've never told is this: I did not cry for Grant. But that baby broke my heart into pieces.

I DRIVE OVER TWO SPEEDBUMPS, onto the campus of ranch-style homes, each brown, nondescript, and labeled. It is nearly 1:00 a.m. when I park in the unpaved back lot of Bright House and walk to the door, the spring night air dampening my face. I do not knock. Inside, the residents are asleep and the house is dim, nightlights dotting the hallway. I smell the citrus air freshener, hear the dryers churning in the laundry room. In the light of the small lamp on the staff desk, I see the phone is back where it belongs.

"I thought you'd come," a woman says, appearing around a corner. It is Marcie, one of the younger ones, putting in her time at the facility until she finishes her psychology degree. She is plump and has a heart tattoo on the inside of her wrist. "Sorry about this," she adds.

I take off my coat and fold it over my arm. I am suddenly overwhelmed with drowsiness. I will be exhausted tomorrow. "Is she okay?" I ask.

"I gave her something to help her sleep."

"This has been happening a lot," I say. "Is something going on?" I recall how upset Fonto was when her favorite staff quit a few years back. How she refused to go to the day program last fall when her summer clothes had been packed away without her knowing.

Marcie turns down the hall toward Fonto's room, and I follow. Her clogs smack the bottoms of her feet as she walks. We come to Fonto's door. It is covered with Fonto's formless paintings, a cardboard heart she covered in glitter blobs for Valentine's Day, a string of bells on the knob. Marcie stops and crosses her arms over her breasts.

"So, I'm not supposed to say anything to you," she says. Her new look of sympathy confuses me. "But the doctor thinks this is dementia. Starting."

"What?" It's all I can say. I know as well as Marcie that people like Fonto are prone to early Alzheimer's, and that the prognosis is worse than in the normal population. Less of a slow decline, more of a walk off a cliff. When Fonto first moved into Bright House, she took the room of another woman who had died of it, the death so fresh that the other residents confused Fonto with the dead one for a few weeks. My mind makes the desperate, irrational connection between the room and the disease. It's the same way I connected, at first, the baby's anatomy to mine, thinking the radiologist had made a mistake and it was my own damaged body on the ultrasound screen and not the fetus. I have the same feeling of being pressed flat into the floor, and I begin to sweat.

Marcie smiles, uncrosses her arms and redoes her ponytail mechanically. She is speaking, and I can tell the words are meant to be comforting, but I hear nothing except the pulsing of blood in my ears. She lets me into Fonto's room. For a moment I stagger forward, lightheaded; it is completely dark in there, as it always is, for Fonto. I switch on the light, see Fonto under the covers in her white daybed, black hair sprayed over the pillow. Her acrylic eyes are open. They are a beautiful amber color, which Nana Hickey picked out to match Fonto's olive skin.

"Hi Quinnie," she says, before I have spoken. Once I thought it was my lavender laundry detergent that gave me away to Fonto and I tried changing it, but no matter the scent of my clothes, Fonto always recognizes me immediately.

"You should be asleep," I say. I sit on the side of her bed and breathe deeply, trying to stop the spinning. The staff is supposed to take her eyes out at night and clean them with baby shampoo, but they forget. The eyes have dots on the back, one for the left eye and two for the right. More than once the staff have put them in the wrong way which makes Fonto look cross-eyed and froggish.

Fonto shifts over. "Nana Hickey wears a Bam-Bam up-do." Her voice is thick. I picture Nana Hickey with the fat bun on top of her head, held in place with a crochet needle. I never knew where Fonto got the term, and yet it seemed to fit.

"Yes, she does."

"What color are carrots? Purple?"

The door is half open, and I can hear Marcie's clogs smacking down the hall. I wonder if I could walk past without her noticing, slip out the side door. I imagine rolling the windows down and turning the radio on, hitting the speed bumps too fast, driving until the sky lightens and I'm too far away to return.

"They're orange," I say.

"Toto makes me cry. Doesn't it, Quinnie?"

I smell her musky body odor and the fruitiness of her dollar store shampoo. The dizziness passes. "You don't care for Toto," I say.

"Lie down," she says.

The heft of my fatigue settles on me. Down the hall, Marcie is heating something up in the microwave. I hear the plastic door slam, and the beeping of the buttons. I lie back, keeping my legs on the floor.

"Tell me what I like," Fonto says.

"You like Paul Simon, and mustard."

"What else?"

"Horses," I say. "Swimming. Orange tea." The bed is softer than my own, warm with Fonto's small heat.

"And Toaster Strudels," she says. "What happens if I eat too many Strudels?"

"You'll get a belly ache."

"And what else do I like?"

"Sweaters, Lionel Richie."

"He has a nice voice, doesn't he?"

"Yes."

"And what else?"

I say all the right things, the way I am supposed to. There is a peace to it, giving in to the script. Fonto's body relaxes. Her breaths lengthen. Her eyelids close over her prosthetics.

For a moment, I allow my eyes to close, as well. I wait for Fonto to say her next line, but nothing comes. She is asleep.

If I wanted, I could leave right now. Fonto would not know. I could go to work in the morning and cancel on Friday and wait for the day Fonto forgets who I am and there is nothing left to hold me down. Without her, I will be so light. I will lift on the breeze and blow away.

But for now, I go on. The list of things Fonto likes is long, and I am the only one who knows the items by heart, and in what order each must come. "Wheel of Fortune, sweatshirts, hot chocolate, Stevie B, pineapple, Burger King French fries," I whisper. Fonto's breaths are drawing in and out of her slack mouth. She doesn't hear me, but it doesn't matter. "Scrambled eggs, velvet chairs, The Golden Girls, donuts. Babies, friends. Love." These are our words. This is how we speak. As long as I am here, I will say my lines. For her, I will say them again, and again, and again.

Acknowledgments

Thanks to the following journals, where earlier versions of these stories first appeared:

"Everyone Is Smiling" in *Hypertext Magazine*.

"The Principle" in *Redivider*.

"Humane" in *Superstition Review*.

"Grace Period" in *The MacGuffin*.

"Distance" under the title "Serious" in *Paradigm Journal*.

"The Battle" in *Ascent*.

"Dysfluency" in *Cumberland River Review*.

"Lucky" in *The Summerset Review*.

"The Visit" in *Blue Lake Review*.

"This Is How We Speak" in *The Boiler*.

"The Natural World" in *MudRoom*.

This collection of stories has taken me an absurdly long time to put together, some of these stories typed with one hand while my other arm held my firstborn—the boy who, this past September, entered his first year of college. Over the years, writing has often taken a backseat to parenting, working, and the other non-negotiables of life, sometimes set aside for months or even years at a time. Through it all, my parents have been my faithful cheerleaders, celebrating even the smallest of my achievements, believing with certainty that I will succeed, and always reflecting back to me the person they believe me to be—a writer. I would have given up long ago if not for them, and I am truly thankful for their support. And right alongside my parents, I must thank my lifelong friend, Shauna Shiff, the girl who won my heart in first grade when she gave me a brown paper bag full of seashells and whose artistic, giving nature has been a constant in my life ever since. Thank you, Shauna, for your astute editorial feedback on these stories (and even suggesting a title for one, which I loved), for inspiring me with your own writing, and for agreeing to take my author photo even though we both know I am the very worst model.

Thank you to publisher Dr. Ross Tangedal, managing editor Brianna Loving, and the wonderful team at Cornerstone Press. I am incredibly humbled to be included in the Legacy Series next to such outstanding, award-winning authors. I am beyond grateful for this opportunity.

Thank you to all my past writing groups—these stories have been through several. Thank you, Colleen Kennedy Pratt, for meeting me at Milano Cafe every month to workshop our writing over coffee, and thank you to my devoted little group from the Cape Cod Writers Center.

And most of all, thank you to my husband, Jay, and our boys, Gabe, Harry, and Oscar. I am so lucky to have you.

REBECCA REYNOLDS holds an MFA from Emerson College and has published stories in *Ascent, MudRoom, Hypertext, The MacGuffin, The Boiler, Eunoia, Copper Nickel, Redivider, Superstition Review, Blue Lake Review, Cumberland River Review,* and elsewhere. She is a guest editor for *The Masters Review* and *CRAFT*, and works at her local public library. She lives with her husband and three sons in a small town south of Boston.

www.ingramcontent.com/pod-product-compliance
Lightning Source LLC
LaVergne TN
LVHW040057080526
838202LV00045B/3682